tex•tu•al

tennison long

Also by the author:

Glorious Verve

When We Ran The Master Plan

Of Tribe & Empire

On Becoming Yesterday's Actors

How to Fake Your Death (& Other Illusions of Exile)

The Devolution

Long Hand Publications

www.tennisonlong.com

ISBN: 9781005846541

Cover Design by Ean Clevenger

This is a work of fiction. Names, characters, places, and incidents are the product of the author's imagination or are used fictitiously, and any resemblance to actual persons, living or dead, events, or locales is entirely coincidental.

For the imaginary friend I never had...

DAY•ZERO

New phone. Who dis?

Oh this could get interesting. How about your worst nightmare?

Two can play this game

I can't believe you already forgot me, was I not that memorable?

Been busy trying to find out if I am going back to work

I know, this whole thing has me worried

It will blow over soon but if we got to stay indoors I need groceries

I got some groceries for you

That is nice and all but I don't know who I am conversating with so

Boo why you gotta play me like that

[new phone, who dis. (slang, humorous) assertion that the recipient of a communication does not recognize the sender of the communication, implying that the sender is insignificant]

DAY•ONE

Everything is changing, and so unexpectedly

Oh you still there?

Ok I will go easy on the requests for nudes

Oh you playin' now

Well I need to know what I'm working with here, ya know

I don't even know who you are

Just play along, it will be fun

Why don't I call this number and expose you for who you are

Go ahead maybe I will answer

[enter *67 and then the number you want to block from seeing your caller ID info; other ways to stop nuisance calls, add your number to the free National Do Not Call Registry by calling 888.382.1222 or going to www.donotcall.gov]

DAY•TWO

Whew, I got out of work, I mean I still gotta work but remotely

At least you got a job

What's up with you?

I don't really want to say but it's up in the air right now

Sorry to hear that but better safe than sorry

Yeah I am getting a little nervous and shit like this don't scare me

I got a relative that works in an ER and they said it's bad

● ● ●

Like a war zone type of thing, folks dying in the lobby

Yes, that's what I'm hearing so I'm glad we got these lockdown orders

14 days should do it

Some much needed time for myself, time for self care

What about self loving?

You had to go there didn't you?

It's not my fault I have a healthy imagination

Well there will be some of that considering I'm all alone up in here

Where is here, exactly?

That, my friend, is going to remain a mystery

For now?

I suppose

• • •

Whatcha making for din?

A big ol salad w ingredients I got at last weekend's farmers market

Oh that sounds healthy

What about you?

Probably a bottle of wine, send pics?

No I rather you try and imagine me from afar

Oh really, then I need clues

So...I am tall

Keep going

Thin, in shape you might call it

I like it

Not your average American fat ass, sorry if you are fat, don't mean to be rude

Keep going

So people tell me I stand out because of my shape

Yeah I think as a country we let shit go too far

I'm not fat shaming, to each his/her own. I can only do me

•   •   •

I heard this virus, or whatever we are calling it, may end up killing millions

I heard that too

But this lockdown, even for 2 weeks might get some ppl so depressed they off themselves

Or gain 20 pounds lol

Yes there is that need for comfort, food and TV

Not my thing really

Have you been watching the news?

As little as possible, mostly out of self preservation

It's bad, I don't mean like the coverage but what's going on

Do tell

Just so many dying, and now all the first responders I'm afraid they are gonna die

They did sign on for that, so not tripping

News coming out of Italy and Spain is devastating

Sorry but I'm worried about my block, and specifically my employment

Yes, it's good to keep perspective

Nighty night

[The intent of this Order is to ensure that the maximum number of people shelter in place in their places of residence to the maximum extent feasible, while enabling essential services to continue, to slow the spread of the outbreak to the maximum extent possible. When people need to leave their places of residence, whether to obtain or perform vital services, or to otherwise facilitate authorized activities necessary for continuity of social and commercial life, they should at all times reasonably possible comply with Social Distancing Requirements. All provisions of this Order should be interpreted to effectuate this intent. Failure to comply with any of the provisions of this Order constitutes an imminent threat to public health]

[All individuals are ordered to shelter at their place of residence. To the extent individuals who are not part of a single household are using shared residential spaces (e.g., common patios, laundry rooms, lobbies), they must at all times as reasonably possible maintain social distancing of at least six feet from any other person]

DAY●THREE

Did you sleep well?

Some nightmares but that's normal at this point in my existence

Did you see the president's presser

No what I miss

He said there may be an existing malaria drug that can kill the virus, we could all go back to work

Yeah well not so fast

But at least it's something good

Yeah but I'm kinda liking this shelter in place thang

It is appealing not rushing out of the house, or having to be somewhere

I like not getting into a car

And pajamas all day

Well, I do shower and shave and don something relaxing

Send pics

It's just yoga pants or other athleisure, nothing too hyped

But I think it's time we exchanged pics

Not so fast cowboy

I need to see what I'm working with

Do you really?

I mean come on, throw me a bone

What about mystery, what about the eroticism of not knowing

Too impatient for that

If you need something you have all the internet porn of the world at your fingertips

• • •

They are saying now that stores have to close this Friday, only groceries will be available

Shit's getting real, what can I say

That the food supply chain is stable and not to hoard food

I'm good over here with my protein shakes, yay

I need to get toilet paper lol before it's all gone

Yeah that wouldn't be good

If I find some you want me to bring it over?

I won't even send you a pic of me, why would I want to meet?

[Athleisure is a fabricated style of clothing typically worn during athletic activities and in other settings, such as at the workplace, at school, or at other casual or social occasions. Athleisure outfits can include yoga pants, tights, sneakers, leggings and shorts, that "look like athletic wear," characterized as "fashionable, dressed up sweats and exercise clothing." The idea is that gym clothes are supposedly making their way out of the gym and becoming a larger part of people's everyday wardrobes. Athleisure can be considered as a fashion industry movement, enabled by improved textile materials, which allow sportswear to be more versatile, comfortable, and fashionable]

[Every second 28,258 internet users are watching pornography; over $3,000 is being spent on access to porn; and 372 people are typing the word "adult" into a search engine]

[Many consumers of toilet paper are going to the bathroom in different locations from before the pandemic - at home instead of workplaces, which often use a different kind of toilet paper than used at home. One kind of bath tissue - for the commercial market - often is made of one ply of recycled fiber and generally is found on rollers at businesses and public places. The other kind - retail toilet paper - is often made of two-ply virgin fiber and is generally much softer for use at home. This location shift prompted by shelter-at-home rules will lead to an estimated 40% increase over the average daily home usage, according to Georgia-Pacific, which makes Quilted Northern toilet paper and other paper products]

DAY•FOUR

Good morning darlin

What up boo?

My building super said we can't have people over

Well I wasn't planning on coming over

I didn't mean for you, just sayin

It's getting real up in this mother fucker

I saw on the news that more than 2mil may die now

And I am over here like waiting for it

You are joking right?

Of course, I mean who is so callous that they would want so much death?

Thank you

For what?

For not being so cold, this is a time of compassion

Yeah but some of this falls into the category, of not my circus, not my monkey

LMFAO

No for real, there is only so much I can take in before it becomes too much

I'm with you but I feel for all these newly minted "essential" workers

Sorry, but who?

Like truckers and supermarket checkers

You think they're all gonna die?

Maybe, it's possible

Then what?

We won't get groceries

And everyone loses a little weight, I see no problem in that

Savage AF, but I like that about you

• • •

So any news for me?

They are saying that we shouldn't wear masks

Why is that?

Cuz they don't work, they make you sicker, and this virus can go right through them

Good cuz I ain't wearing one

They said it can give a false sense of safety too

Oh like condoms?

I guess, it makes you feel like you can get closer than 6 feet to a stranger

Oh my bad

That you feel invincible to the hidden enemy

Well we are coming on a week of lockdown and I haven't left the house

If you don't need to then please don't, it's cray cray out there

There is something about Americans, it's a strange mix of smart ppl and dumb mfers

Yes there is some of that going on

It's just going to get worse the longer this goes on

Well I hope it's over sooner than later

Not me, I kinda like it

But then we can finally meet

Not necessarily

● ● ●

Hey you there?

What now

I saw that if your underwear and jeans can't hold back a fart how is a mask up for the task

That's funny, so true

That's it, night

[Ferguson/Imperial College Code models indicated that the virus, if left entirely unmitigated, could kill in the order of two million citizens over the next year and that ICUs would be stretched beyond capacity. Advisory teams discussed suppressing the pandemic by social distancing, but officials are worried that this would only lead to a bigger second outbreak later in the year]

[Not my circus, not my monkey. Language: Polish; Translation: Nie mój cyrk, nie moje malpy; Meaning: Not my problem]

[Almost everyone would say their work is essential for some reason, but because of the pandemic's immediate threat to human life, essential work is now widely understood as work deemed necessary to meet basic needs of human survival and well-being — food, health, safety and cleaning]

[Savage AF brings together two slang terms. The first is savage, which has meant "brutal" or "aggressive" since the 1500s. From the 1990s and on, savage has also been slang for "excellent" (à la fierce or wicked), it has also come to describe a remark as hilariously but ruthlessly on point. The second is AF, often lowercased as af and standing for as fuck. As fuck is an intensifying phrase used since the late 1970s. It's been abbreviated, and mildly censored, as AF in text messages and on social media since the late 2000s. Early uses of savage AF describe something as extremely good, a use that continues today]

[The most dangerous aspect of masks is psychological, allowing people to enter a fantasy of normality even when we are far from it. Considering the public cannot use manufactured equipment correctly, one must ask how the fundamentally inferior homemade masks will compare. Without additional filters, cotton masks are only 4.5 % as effective at protecting the wearer as surgical masks, which are themselves, equally inferior to N95s]

[cray cray: a reference to the schizophrenic crime lord twins Ronald and Reginald Kray of 1950s London. Brought into its current usage by the Jay Z lyric, "Ball so hard, muthafuckas wanna find me, that shit Kray. That shit Kray. That shit Kray"]

[The highly infectious virus is spread via aerosols (droplets of saliva or nasal discharge spread by coughing or sneezing by the infected person with the mouth uncovered), yet new speculation reveals that it could spread via fecal matter and even via flatulence]

DAY●FIVE

So my work called and they are making me work from home

That's good, no?

Yes at least I'm not furloughed

What do you do, if I may ask?

Lately I been running a hot text line

Oh you call this hot?

It can be as hot as you want

I am waiting for the goods

Keep waiting boo

Just send me a teaser, something to work with here

You don't even know me, what if I am a beast?

Do it for the sake of quarantine charity

Even if I send you something how will you know it's me

Well isn't that part of the thrill

I suppose I could pose for you with something you request

Now we are talking

Like in a red thong

Keep going

Or like a hostage I could stand there with a copy of today's paper

I prefer the thong scenario, any color really

Well see that would be nothing more than a big tease

But I'm asking so I am a willing participant

Let me think on it, the more you ask the slimmer your odds

● ● ●

Hey, did you see the news?

No what is it now

That all of this started from a bat soup

Wtf is that?

Peeps in China eating soup made of bats

Oh hell no

Yes and somehow that bat meat turns into a virus in humans

Umkay

They get these exotic animals at places called 'wet markets'

Gross

Yeah you can buy things like live penguins

Ok I'm out, night

[Bat Soup Recipe: place the bats in a large kettle and add water, ginger, onion, garlic and salt. Bring to a boil and cook for 60 minutes. Strain broth into a second kettle. Take the bats, skin them and discard the skin. Remove meat from the bones and return meat, and any of the viscera you fancy, to the broth. Heat. Serve liberally sprinkled with scallions and further seasoned with soy sauce and/or coconut cream. Makes 4 servings]

[Somewhat akin to farmer's markets and found around the world, wet markets are typically large collections of open-air stalls selling fresh seafood, meat, fruits, and vegetables.

Some wet markets sell and slaughter live animals on site, including chickens, fish, and shellfish. Also some sell wild animals for their meat, with selections that include snakes, bats, beavers, penguins, porcupines, and baby crocodiles, among other animals]

DAY•SIX

Good morning

So nice outside, it's a shame we can't go out

Doesn't seem like a good idea

The virus?

Word on the news is that it lingers on surfaces of everything for weeks

So like if you touch anything you gonna get it?

Yes, it's spreading on boxes delivered at houses, even sometimes on the to-go food

I haven't ordered any yet

And then there is like a radius spread, where if someone coughs it could infect an entire large room

So you're saying this is bad

Yes worse than bad

This month already feels lost to me, idk what day it even is

It's Friday

Thanks for that, you sure?

Yes cuz it's trash day, I put my cans out, with gloves!

Ok good boy

Yeah I don't need you coming after me about my hygiene

Gross

Btw I am a very clean person already

Like what?

Like several showers a day, washing my hands, manscaping

Well good on you, but this should be expected

I'm just saying, in case you are wondering

Well I wasn't but I'm happy for you

Why you always gotta have that tone with me?

What tone?

That tone

Go get some fresh air, I'm out

•   •   •

Hey sorry about earlier

What?

The whole tone conversation

Ok

I think this being lockdown is getting to me

Do it for the elderly they said

It seems that we have to flatten the curve to keep the hospitals ready

I heard that too but I don't know about that

Watcha mean?

My friend's cousin is a nurse and said the hospitals got cleared out and haven't seen anyone

Like they are empty?

Yes, granted it's early but what if it doesn't happen

I am thinking that the first to die will be the homeless

Those fools are hardened

Yes but they are clustered together

Then there will be a cull

Like a slaughter of wild animals

Yes, but in nature, by nature, bat soup to indigent slaughter

Yikes

The politicians aren't doing anything about it so the only hope is nature

Good point there

These folks are lost souls, missing from family

Yes but sometimes it's just they need a house

Not within the confines of a schizophrenic firestorm going off in their minds

Then they need help

It could be beyond that

Then leave them out there to the elements

Hey many want to be there?

I think the govt can do more

Too corrupt, they already use homelessness as a vehicle for corruption

• • •

Hot topic go

Your raging sex drive?

Good guess

I'm not gonna sext you so give it up boo

What if I send you something?

Then you may never hear from me again

What if it's something you are guaranteed to like

You still run the risk

That's interesting

It might be deuces

Ok let me think on it

No rush, I'm warning you

• • •

They say on the news that 2mil might die

Scary numbers

That it's like 1918

Well they gotta sell ads

Whatcha mean

The news, they sell ads to run their programs

And?

So their content needs to get eyeballs

Yes but they can't just make stuff up

Oh yes they can

But they would get in trouble

By who? Get real. This convo is showing some ignorance on your end

I'm sorry

Don't be sorry, just don't believe everything you see

[The girl responds in a very innocent manner or smiles a little bit (not grin or giggle or laugh) and says IDK. In texting it means yes but she wants you to ask again and be more straight forward this time. Sometimes IDK means she wants you (strictly for bf or very very close friend) to figure it out by yourself]

[In epidemiology, the idea of slowing a virus' spread so that fewer people need to seek treatment at any given time is known as "flattening the curve." It explains why the government is implementing social distancing guidelines, including the shelter in place orders]

[cull: a selective slaughter of wild animals]

[sext: to send someone a sexually explicit message or image by cell phone; to engage in sexting]

[deuces: African American vernacular, slang meaning peace; goodbye (because of the associated gesture holding up two fingers)]

[The Spanish flu, also known as the 1918 flu pandemic, was an unusually deadly influenza pandemic caused by the H1N1 influenza A virus. Lasting about 15 months from spring 1918 to early summer 1919, it infected 500 million people, about a third of the world's population at the time]

DAY●SEVEN

So I went out today and did yoga by myself in the park

Nice how was it?

Blissful and much needed

Did you wear yoga pants

Yes and I thought of you when I was putting them on

For reals?

Yes the clean ones from my laundry were a bit tighter to squeeze on

And?

So it means I gained a little over the last week, mostly in the ass dept

A visual would really help right now

And then they were more constraining when I went into child's pose from downward dog

Is that the position?

Yes collapsed doggy style kinda

I'm sure you looked great

Half of it is about how you look

Which park?

Many of the yoga bitches I know are all about the expensive brands like it helps you get better

Can I guess?

They don't even know how to do the poses, it's all about the social media check in and the pictures they take

I get tired of that stuff, glad to hear you're not like that

It's like they are doing it half ass just for the online acknowledgment

Yes, twisted

As if another like or heart sign will justify their existence of failure

Sad stuff if you think about it

Kinda like looking for meaning that isn't there, filling an emptiness

That's why I never really got into social media

So much of it is daddy issues really

Are you close with your dad?

Daddy issues that propel a youthful hatred, or even distrust in men, into adulthood and that simmering underlying anger manifested in your own need to feel admonished

So take back that last question

And then you realize you kinda need men but they are fully vilified in your mind so you try and balance out the equation

Yeaah I get it

But then you know you won't really make it work with other women, like an actual relationship

Yes

Like two women together eventually get catty, and cycle together

I can't imagine

Then the stark reality that you're gonna miss cock

Oh?

And there are lots of redeeming qualities to men if you can see through your own issues

Thanks, I do think we deserve more credit

So you don't need to go full gamma male on me to try and get my sympathy

Excuse me, did I say anything?

Just don't preach me any bullshit about the sexes, been hearing it all my life

Ok

I know men and women serve their own purposes in the world

Ok

I'm just saying many of those who are easily triggered likely have daddy issues because I have been there myself

[The void social media fills is the motivation for instant gratification, and the idea that bigger and better will bring about happiness. This influences how and what people share on social media sites, resulting in users constantly comparing themselves to others and thinking less of their own lives, potentially leading to negative feelings such as jealousy or low self-esteem]

[Daddy issues is an informal phrase for the psychological challenges resulting from an absent or abnormal relationship with one's father, often manifesting in a distrust of, or sexual desire for, men who act as father figures]

[Period syncing is also known as "menstrual synchrony" and "the McClintock effect." It's based on the theory that when you come in physical contact with another person who menstruates, your pheromones influence each other so that eventually your monthly cycles line up]

[Gamma Males: Introspective, unusual, unattractive, and all too often bitter, gammas tend to be intelligent, yet unsuccessful with women, and not uncommonly all but invisible to them. They alternate between placing women on pedestals and hating the entire sex]

DAY●EIGHT

They are saying this is like 10 times deadlier than the flu

Who, the news?

Well yes

I told you about them

I know but c'mon, their job is to spread the information

Or misinformation, worse than the virus itself

So who should I trust?

Idk, have you ever relied on your own instincts?

Sometimes but honestly I end up questioning myself

That's called impostor syndrome

So you're saying I'm an imposter now?

No the syndrome is called that when people are in a position to effectively make a decision on their own but they begin to question themselves, this even happens w surgeons and commercial pilots

Well isn't it normal to an extent

Yes I suppose, as a way to have our reptilian brains sense potential danger as an outcome from a decision

So we should listen to this 'sense'

To a degree but then you need to make stronger decisions and proceed, otherwise you remain crippled by the indecision, or held back by always taking the safe route

How does this apply to the news

You got to ingest it w a grain of salt then make your own calculations based on your gut and life experiences

Interesting

Not really. It comes down to your world view, all the events of your life leading up to this moment now. That's why we have leftists and extreme right leaning ppl. It's not that any one viewpoint is right or wrong because it's based on life experiences. Then compound that with emotional fortitude

• • •

You still there?

When you add in the trauma of life, it comes down to how/if it was processed. The devil always includes the details. You can process the pain, grow with it, take on the scar tissue, or repel it, build walls around yourself, self-isolate. Then when it's go time you're either a warrior or a worrier. Am I getting too deep for you?

No please go on.

Gently reclines into armchair psychologist's chair, and you take these missives to be terms of endearment for some, and for others signs of weakness. Lost in the grander big picture equation is that we need the weak as much as we need the

48

strong. There can be neither side if it is all blended into the same pathos

I can't wait for the day we can have these conversations over a nice glass of cab

When we hit the pause button on our feelings, this is kinda what you get, a bunch of ppl hiding out in their apartments waiting for the fear to subside...but it's not going anywhere cuz the fear is inside you

[Impostor Syndrome (also known as impostor phenomenon, impostorism, fraud syndrome or the impostor experience) is a psychological pattern in which one doubts one's accomplishments and has a persistent internalized fear of being exposed as a fraud]

[The reptilian brain, composed of the basal ganglia (striatum) and brainstem, is involved with primitive drives related to thirst, hunger, sexuality, and territoriality, as well as habits and procedural memory (like putting your keys in the same place every day without thinking about it or riding a bike). Many people call it the Lizard Brain, because the limbic system is about all a lizard has for brain function. It is in charge of fight, flight, feeding, fear, freezing up, and fornication]

[Pathos, or the emotional appeal, means to persuade an audience by appealing to their emotions]

DAY●NINE

There are reports coming out that the numbers may be wrong

Well, good morning

Sorry, hello

What numbers?

That the fatality rates are not in line with the number of infected, factored into numbers of those tested

Wtf does all of that mean?

It gets confusing, but if I understand it right, there are more ppl than they originally thought that have had it, and obviously survived

So that's a good thing? You saw that on your news?

And what is happening under those numbers is that the death rate would collapse downward, in fact it would make this virus less fatal than the anal flu

Ha, you said anal

Maybe I slipped that in there to see if you were reading

Well check your sources boo, that sounds too rosy for the mainstream narrative

It could mean we all go back to work sooner than not

And this idea excites you?

Excite is not the word but I think it may be good for us

What if I told you I like this break

That's on you boo, I ain't hatin'

Why you got to switch into black voice?

Sorry just trying to sound cool

• • •

They just came out with a rumor that the lockdowns may be extended another 15 days

Who says, the news?

Yes who else?

Bye boy

What did I say now?

Your tone

Sorry

And affect in your message

I'm sorry

Why you got to believe everything you read?

I mean it's news after all

Don't you see there may be something else behind it

Like what?

Like a certain narrative may need to be set in order to attain a desired outcome

Okay

Like you when you talk to me, you are massaging the messenger just so that I might come around to sending you a nude

Okay yes I get it

So you have a pussy agenda and whether you consciously go for it or not you are after it

Well I wouldn't call it all a pussy agenda

Then what really? What more do you want from me?

I enjoy our chats

But with the idea that it leads to more

I suppose

Don't lie to yourself, it's not a good look

Sorry

And don't apologize every time I critique your approach

Okay

So if pussy is your end goal, and for most men this is the deal,
then you need to set the scenario of how to get there

Any insight would be appreciated

I'm not here to tell you how, I'm just saying the news has its
own intentions aligned along similar structures, to get there
they need to bring the people along

But what's in it for them?

Could be many things. Self preservation comes to mind.
Ratings. Maybe even to maintain a cover up for something
bigger we cannot imagine

Ha, now you are sounding like a conspiracy theorist

[affect: transitive verb; to produce an effect upon: such as to
produce a material influence upon or alteration; to act upon (a
person, a person's mind or feelings, etc.) so as to effect a
response; or influence, to be greatly affected by the terrible
news]

[pussy agenda, aka vagenda, when a man is so driven by
pussy his mission is solely based on its attainment; inversely it

can be defined as a tool used by women to obtain their own agenda]

[conspiracy theorist: the CIA invented the term in 1967 to disqualify those who questioned the official version of John F Kennedy's assassination and doubted that his killer, Lee Harvey Oswald, had acted alone. Another side-effect of this new stigma was that the label conspiracy theory or theorist became a pejorative term. The Kennedy assassination was the first major instance in which conspiracy theorists accused the state of secretly plotting evil and provided alternative accounts that were then labelled conspiracy theories. So it is hardly surprising that conspiracy theorists, who blame events on the intentional actions of evil people, retrospectively see the emergence of the term as a deliberate attempt to uphold the official version of the Kennedy assassination]

DAY●TEN

Lesson for the day, don't call anyone a conspiracy theorist then expect to keep an intelligent conversation going

I'm sorry about that

And dial back the apologies

Throwing around 'conspiracy theorist' discredits the beliefs of individuals who may simply be free thinking. Having thoughts outside of what is being pushed down their throats, seeing there may be a third or fourth, or twentieth side to every story. Or that the real story is not the one you are focussing in on but something else that "they" don't want you to know about

I would joke that my tin foil hat is now on, teacher

Keep joking and I will block your ass lmfao

Ha, you wrote lmfao. I admit that makes me feel a bit better, knowing you have a sense of humor

It's not really humor but a sense of frivolity, meaning I don't take this shit as seriously as you do, or as seriously as you think I should be

[free thinking, or freethought, is an epistemological viewpoint which holds that positions regarding truth should be formed only on the basis of logic, reason, and empiricism, rather than authority, tradition, revelation, or dogma]

[LMFAO: internet slang, vulgar, initialism of laughing my fucking ass (arse) off]

DAY•ELEVEN

"They" are now saying that there could be a tsunami of mental illness after the lockdown, or even during it

Like the weak fucks are gonna lose it even more?

I guess that is what they are saying

Could it just be that conditions like this, and the fear machine have amplified what's already fucked up in people's minds

I guess but I can't relate, it seems to me that I am boring when compared to how the minds of others work

Oh aren't you special

It's not that but I rack my brain trying to find out if my thoughts appear to be anything but normal, like abnormal desires or spin away thinking patterns and I don't see it

Well is a fish aware of water?

Like you mean I may be crazy and not know it

Yes, within the confines of your own mind how would you know?

Does extreme horniness count?

Yes, if you are using that as fuel to some other end goal

Does a lingering childhood desire to please my mother count?

Yes, very much so

Does a sense of inferiority when it comes to my own looks count?

It could but I don't know what you are working with

I could send you a selfie

But I wouldnt know if it was in fact you

I'm not a catfish

Not saying that but without the IRL interaction it's all a facade show piece of life

Can I tell you something?

Fire away

Something that does concern me is that even though I am an adult sometimes I feel like I am just the little boy that I was decades ago, that I'm still that child but now living within the body of this man

You mean like arrested development?

I don't know what that is

Kinda like you stopped developing emotionally at some point, but your body kept developing

Yes, and with it comes the insecurities, that I am an impostor, that I don't have all those manly qualities that the advertisements and magazines expect

Just do you

Sometimes though it's crippling

How so?

Sorry I think I am going off on a tangent here

No it's all good, I'm not going anywhere today

Lol, it's just that I don't feel fully enough. Like from the confidence of men I see, those w children and beautiful wives, or the rich dudes in their fancy cars, even the guys in porn with the big dicks. I think collectively it's like a tidal wave of inferiority that becomes me

So you're saying you are working with a small dick?

Oh, um, no, but in comparison to some I see in porn I'm like wtf. I can sort and reason that of course they need big dicks on film, it's not like ppl want to watch small dicks. And the camera angles work in their favor

Stop comparing yourself to others, it's that simple

But I can't stop, it's like I need a gauge to compare myself against. Some standard or ideal

Well maybe for once make your own self the ideal. You find advancement in the small steps you make each day. If you want to look better do something about it. If you don't like seeing big dicks stop watching porn. If you want the kids and wife then take steps to get there

I don't mean to be such a downer so early in the morning. Btw good morning!

You know the expression, how do you eat an elephant?

No, how?

One bite at a time

• • •

There is this fire spreading w the virus across the Mediterranean and all I can say is maybe it's the fact that everyone lives together. And they smoke. And nobody will acknowledge that they don't have the medical health system that we have. Somewhat of a perfect storm really

So it's not going to do us like that?

My suspicion is not. But the news says it will be worse. The 2 mil dead maybe even be recalculated upward

The old people?

No this would include everyone, even the children and healthy young people

Oh that is not good

A teenage girl died of it, she was homecoming queen, healthy, then one night told her mom she wasn't feeling too good, went to bed and they found her dead in the morning

Wow, that is sad

So maybe it's good we are all keeping our distance

But what happens when this is over and we go back to regularly scheduled programming

We will have a vaccine by then

But what if we don't

We will

We don't have a vaccine for AIDS or ebola

Good point

I was reading H1N1, it just went away on its own

Well I think this virus is different, as nasty as it is I trust the doctors will get it right

I like your confidence but sadly I think you are too optimistic

• • •

They are saying late summer we should have something

Like a cure?

Yes and we can restart the economy and everything will be back to normal

Except my waistline

Well I'm sure that's not a bad thing

I admit I rather enjoy the solitude

I'm getting ancy

Take this time to look inward, to find yourself, to wonder why you are so crazy

You think I'm crazy now?

We all are, don't be ashamed

I guess I need to accept it

If you do not acknowledge the disease you cannot cure it

[catfish: an internet predator that fabricates online identities and entire social circles to trick people into emotional/romantic relationships. Possible motivations: revenge, loneliness, curiosity, boredom]

[IRL: abbreviation for In Real Life. Often used in internet chat rooms to let people know you are talking about something in the real world and not in the internet world]

[arrested development: the roots of Arrested Psychological Development are from past traumas or disturbances in childhood, adolescence or one's family of origin, specifically to problems in the parent-child relationship in each childhood developmental stage. It is believed that narcissistic personality disorder is created before a child turns three years old. This early origin is thought to explain why narcissists are so difficult to treat in later adult life, and is the reason that some adults act like children emotionally]

DAY•TWELVE

Do you ever question how we as humans adapted so quickly to these new rules of life?

Yes, we are just good at adapting

And terms like social distancing that literally have been around for a minute now all up in our vocabularies

We do well at conforming

But why are we so chill with it?

Because it's what we have to do to flatten the curve

But that is what they are telling us. Nobody is questioning the authority

If we all just play our small role in this we will be out of it soon enough

It's that mindset that worries me

If we are selfish then it just sets back the cause

Yes, that attitude is what should concern even yourself

It's about life versus death at this point

But not if the cure is worse than the disease

Idk I'm ok with doing my part

[the cure is worse than the disease: The medical treatment for an illness produces a worse net result than the illness does (threatens a non-negligible risk of doing so), especially via adverse effects. Figuratively, the solution or proposed solution to a problem produces a worse net result than the problem does (threatens a non-negligible risk of doing so), especially via unintended consequences]

DAY•THIRTEEN

But when we go back out do we just get it anyway?

Good morning

Like this talk of herd immunity, it can't happen if we are isolated

When we come out there will be a cure

If no cure comes we will still need to come out, and then it could spread, like wildfire, like originally how nature had intended it to, but this time on a population with weakened immune systems

I'm just saying there should be a vaccine

But what if there is not, how long can we go sheltering in place? The low grade constant stresses are eating at my immune system. I feel weaker, I need my gym time. And I miss sitting in the sun for my vitamin D. I'm not even gonna bring up all the overweight people

Yes, that's a factor, what they are calling 'comorbidities' as additional reasons or contributing factors to why someone dies of it

And so if you are healthy and you get the virus your chance of survival is like 99 percent?

Maybe like 80 percent. Like 8 out of 10 would survive. I know you would

Thanks boo. Isn't the average death age like 80? Can you check that fact Mr Factchecker

I dont think it's that high but yes, elderlies

And then if they are dying of cancer, let's say, then they get the virus, and die it gets counted as a virus death?

Yes because it is a virus death

But doesn't this play with the numbers a little?

Maybe the coroners and doctors are just being honest

And let's say you are morbidly obese, like 200 pounds overweight, you got all kinds of issues like sleep apnea, fat pressuring down on your organs and lungs, maybe even add in you are a heavy smoker, now you get it and die

It would be the virus that got you

Are you playing dumb or just playing along?

I'm following

So my question is are these comorbidities ready to take the ppl out anyway? Like they would have died without the virus, and it's just govt counting the deaths so for some other reason

The news did say that hospitals get $39k if they hook someone with the virus up to a ventilator

Then follow the money son

[herd immunity: when most of a population is immune to an infectious disease, this provides indirect protection, or herd immunity (also called herd protection), to those who are not immune to the disease]

[comorbidity is the presence of one or more additional conditions often co-occurring with a primary condition, and describes the effect of all other conditions an individual patient might have other than the primary condition of interest, either physiological or psychological]

DAY●FOURTEEN

I was telling this friend of mine that I think I may have already had the virus

Who are you talking to other than me? LOL

I know ppl, you arent my only worldly outlet

Is it bad that I'm kinda jealous

Well it's not one of those things, strictly platonic

Ok just making sure you're not straying on me

And I was saying that about four months ago I had all the symptoms. Regular flu like but then the loss of smell and severe throat irritation

But it wasn't here four months ago

I know that is what they are saying but what I am telling you is that I cannot deny the fact of what I went through

Yes but this is something else

But what if it's the same thing

It's not

But if it is then I have this elusive 'antibody' and it means I can't get it again

Negative, you can still get it again

[Postmortem testing indicates that two people who mysteriously died in their homes months ago were infected with the virus that now has shut down the nation, the county medical examiner has declared. This new information, combined with antibody testing results, suggests that the virus was circulating in this country for at least a month before it first came to light, during the earliest cluster of infection]

[antibodies, also known as immunoglobulins, are Y-shaped proteins that are produced by the immune system to help stop intruders from harming the body. When an intruder enters the body, the immune system springs into action. These invaders, which are called antigens, can be viruses, bacteria, or other chemicals]

DAY•FIFTEEN

So this time 2 weeks ago I had very different plans for my day

Oh yeah?

Yes, some me time - nails, gym, juice, hot yoga, epson bath

I like the visual

Maybe a massage then a couple glasses of cab

And would this be alone or w someone of interest

Why, you jealous now?

No I just need to recreate the scene for my own purposes

It could be me just self loving if you know what I mean

Yes, duly noted...

I don't always need a man to fulfill my needs

So this evening ends with you pleasuring yourself?

It usually does, yes

Well that turns me on immensely I must say

As it should

Thinking of you all worked up from the day to then relieve some pressure

It is all about the build up

Oh believe me I know

And the lead up to it all, setting the pace and laying out how the day will unfold to that final moment

What do you think about when you pleasure yourself?

It's always something different

Like a scene of you there in a room w a strange man?

No, it could be me with a composite of men who are manhandling me roughly

Oh...

Or it could be something more sensual, maybe just the sensations of fingertips running the length of my backside

Uhum

Or the weight of an unknown man, big and strong, mounted atop me and having his way

So it varies?

Absolutely, I mean aren't you like that too?

I don't think guys are like that. I go for what works. The things that I like I then imagine or seek out online

Like casual hookups?

Oh god no, I mean I can look for it in porn

Oh you are one of those guys

What, porn guys?

Yes, that have killed off their real life abilities by flooding their dopamine channels with visual lust

Wouldn't say it has destroyed me, as I am aware of its effects

That's good, I knew a guy once, good looking guy, he couldn't get it up with me

Well that would never be a problem between us

How do you know, you don't even know what I look like

Well I have a good idea and lets just say my instincts are usually right

So this guy was young and he resorted to popping viagra, said he had some dick injury but I knew better and I didn't allow it to bother me, in that I knew it wasn't me

Lol some dudes are idiots

Girls can get self conscious about it - as teenagers we tease each other about pussies smelling like fish

I'm sure that is not your situation

No but the hint of concern lingers, when a guy goes down on you for the first time it's unnerving

It can be like that for guys too

What, gettin your dick sucked or eating the pussy?

Getting sucked, you get nervous that she doesn't know what she is doing and that you might lose your wood

I have always been complimented on my certain skill set for oral

Yeah no complaints for me either

So now that we have established our oral front, what you got planned for today?

[Sexual behavior activates the same 'reward system' circuitry in the brain as addictive drugs, such as cocaine and methamphetamines, which can result in self-reinforcing activity, or recurrent behaviors. Internet pornography has been shown to be a supernormal stimulus of this circuitry, which may be due to the ability to continuously and instantaneously self-select novel and more sexually arousing images. Watching too much internet porn can increase a person's tolerance, the same as with narcotics. Regular watchers of porn are less likely to respond to real-world sexual activity and must increasingly rely on pornography for release]

DAY•SIXTEEN

You want to hear something sick?

Well good morning to you

The virus may not have come from a bat but instead from someone eating a penguin

Oh that is disgusting

Yeah these wet markets are fucking gross

Like, um, where do they get these animals?

Probably some trader dudes that go out and get them

How do these folks acquire a taste for penguins?

Yes so many questions

No for real, how do you know to eat that?

Some raw savage desire

And so this is how we got into this mess?

Yes like AIDS when the Belgian spelunker had sex with a monkey

WTF?

Some things we should not eat, and certainly sex on

I lived through the AIDS pandemic as someone who only had straight sex but I was still scared AF

I hope this one doesn't come to that

Some article I saw from Australia says you can get this virus from farts

Oh for real?

Yes it gets crazy, so the fart would have to be directly from the anus into the recipient's mouth

Ok

Like if it goes through your panties and pants somehow that kills it

So as long as nobody is direct farting into mouths we good?

And now they say it can live in semen

I don't know how much to believe now, it's like there is a constant slew of new details emerging that feed into the fear machine

My thing is this, if only a small percentage of what they are saying is true it is still too much, we are doomed

But maybe that is what they are trying to do, to scare you

For what end goal?

Into submission, into watching their programming

Do they want us to never see each other, live in lockdown forever?

Maybe, as a way to instill something else, or to wreak havoc

But that would be evil

Who said the powers that be are a benevolent lot?

Well the people won't stand much more, they will rise up to any form of tyranny

I can hope, we can hope

[When wildlife are stressed, farmed in small cages and kept in close contact with humans during the entire wet market rearing and slaughtering process, the risk of disease transmission rises. When a pathogen challenges a healthy immune system, the body responds with inflammation to fight it. But when an animal is stressed, the hormone cortisol is released which causes the normal inflammatory response to change into a more limited activation of white blood cells, allowing new pathogens to survive and multiply]

[Natural transfer is the most accepted theory for the origin of HIV. It is proposed that a hunter or bushmeat seller who had skinned or butchered a chimpanzee somewhere in west-central Africa became infected with a simian immunodeficiency virus (SIV), and that this gave birth to the HIV variant (HIV-1 Group M) which has now infected more than 50 million persons worldwide, causing 16 million deaths from AIDS]

DAY●SEVENTEEN

I was thinking last night that if I could live through AIDS I can live through this

Were you that scared?

We did think we were all gonna get it

And then only gays got it?

Yes, I was young, but there was a narrative that straight ppl were dying as much as gay guys

Now we know differently

It was all about the abusive anal sex, tearing fissures and rupturing blood vessels

Straight sex didn't involve blood

But this virus now is airborne

I'm not talking about this virus

Sorry my bad

And the psychology behind the fear of AIDS slowed down a generation's worth of sex, probably making us harder people

I don't think I am much younger than you

And we looked back on free love, on the 60s, on key parties, on the disco scene and were so envious of the casual sex

Every era has its own identity

Then AIDS hits and we shut it down. Now we self regulate from the fear

Like an invisible boogie man?

Yes exactly. You might meet someone at a bar and think do they have it. You might look for signs on their body like a scab or a wound. Tells of the disease. They said even with condoms you could get it. The only way for 100 percent protection was full abstinence

When did things turn?

I don't think there was a particular event. Maybe Magic Johnson. I think ppl figured it out on their own. They didn't see their friends dying. They didn't see celebrities dying. That is the litmus test. And an innate instinct to get back to

business because everything we had seen ran contrary to
what we were being told

• • •

Did you work out tonight?

You mean yoga in my living room in dirty leggings, yes

I don't know why this sounds so hot to me

Because you are nasty

I never saw an ass in leggings I didn't like. Except for at Wal-Mart

They are high tech now, not so much leggings but yoga pants.
And expensive

Sometimes I see an ass that doesnt match the rest of the body

There is that, well-designed to push and pull various parts of
the glutes

It's not fair til men have something like this to emphasize their package

You could always pack a sock in there

Can you imagine the let down in the reveal of pulling down your pants to have a sock fall out

Same for these women who are packing their flabby asses into padded pants, all tight and proper then plop it goes

I like what I see to be as close to the real product as possible

Me too, we are deep into an age of artifice

Are you finally coming around to the level of fake we are enduring?

What do you mean, coming around? I always been skeptical

Thank you for validating my own concerns for what's going on

What now?

The virus, the response, the perceptions, the plan or lack thereof

I tell you it's getting old. But there is a mix of sweet and sour, like some aspects of isolation I like, I also like not having plans when I wake up. But I miss the bustle of the day to day, and as bitchy as I sound I miss being around people

I'm with you on that. Maybe now would be a good time to plan our break from quarantine and meet up. It could even be in a park. It doesnt need to involve sex lol

Wow, you went straight there. What makes you think I am going to put others at risk for your quick burst of satisfaction in meeting up with me. It isn't all about you, even if you think it's fake, you can still harm others

Sorry

Don't be sorry but have some damn compassion for others

I wasn't thinking

Oh yes you were, thinking w your dick again

It's all good, sorry

We have never even met. I could be some big fat man troll, trolling you from a block away or even the other side of the world. You have no verification

I trust it's you. Just call it my inherent ability to see through these things. There is no question you are a woman, and from everything else I surmise an attractive one, just below middle age

Well you are confident, I will give you that

Yes ma'am

[HIV is sexist: a woman is twice as likely to catch the virus from an infected partner in a heterosexual relationship than a man is, and homosexual men are at even greater risk, more than 20 times as likely to get infected from an HIV-positive partner than partners in a heterosexual relationship]

[yoga pant technology: anti-cellulite high waisted leggings that bring versatility with slimming, push up and a textured design, intended to hide the appearance of cellulite and imperfections, while featuring an improved silhouette, thanks to the extremely elastic compressed fabric. Made from technical sculpting fabric, legs and butt will never be the same, with the perfect textured pattern to mask any cellulite and the compression lifting fabric to better sculpt curves, they perform for all activities whether it's hanging out around the house or going out for a workout]

[troll: (noun) was originally a mythical ugly creature, now it usually means an intentionally disruptive person on the internet. Baiting people online came to be known as trolling because the people doing the trolling were considered to be ugly people]

DAY●EIGHTEEN

Can I assume you are in yoga pants this morning?

That would be a safe guess, but it's too easy

Give me something harder

Pun intended?

Are you wearing a bra? What color?

You obviously have never lived with a woman

Why is that?

Bc you would know there is no way in hell I would be lounging around my apartment alone w a bra on - haven't worn one for weeks

Must feel good

It does

Free the titty, save the city

Something like that - they aren't that big so I don't really need a bra, but big enough that my nips can get hard in public and go full high beams on a stranger

Do tell

Tell what, that's it

I guess men do really have it easier in so many ways

Yes I would say so - but y'all got your own issues

Like?

Higher rates of suicide, toxic masculinity, mommy issues

There is that

And the pressure to never show your cards, that certain societal discomfort w being able to express yourself

Yeah women can just get drunk and cry it out

(Laughing) but men when they are at their snapping point like to shoot up public places

Not all of us

No, but how many women go on rampages?

Some but not that many - remember the Iranian girl who went to youtube HQ to kill everyone?

No, wtf?

She had her own youtube channel, some goofy videos of her dancing, and they throttled her exposure, so her viewer numbers collapsed, she drove up from So Cal with a pistol, and began shooting at ppl outside their HQ but then quickly turned the gun on herself

That's awful, but it's telling that ppl can let their own false sense of fame get to their heads

I think the male version of this is the incel

What is that, I mean I heard the term before

Involuntary celibate - INCEL - dudes that can't get laid who then somehow latch onto the identity

Why can't they get laid?

Think fat, gross dudes, then next level those who live w mommy, or are so isolated from society they just cannot fathom any contact w the opposite sex

That's sad

They even have their own groups, boastful societies where they bask in the glory of being incel

Wtf?

And they run w political theories that the govt should mandate women give them sex

Ok now you're playin

No for real, straight up misogynistic logic that we should have sex farms where they can go and have their desires met

How about losing some weight and getting out more

I think it's beyond that for them. There is a sense of doubling down on their original mistakes. The bad decisions that got them to where they are become placeholders for their heightened sense of self, fresh launching off points toward the new identity

Sounds like megalomania

In a way it is. Online they find validation when they seek out others like themselves and come upon ppl that make them feel less alone. Their crazy ideas somehow become justified

You seem to know alot about these guys

I'm not one, I just find it fascinating

Whoa I didn't imply you are one, but now I'm wondering

Please never, this is an insult

Sorry boo just cautious

● ● ●

I looked up the incels

What'd you find?

They are some sick dudes - if you are one, for your own sake, stop thinking like that

Oh hell no I'm not

I'm just saying, it's not a healthy viewpoint - at this point I care about you and just letting you know it's not normal, as much as they try and make it seem so

Well I'm not so let's drop it

Just sayin' - don't be so defensive, makes you look guilty

For what, being an incel?

For covering up something

Like what?

Have you ever had sex? Are you a virgin?

What kind of question is that?

See, like that - deflection

No I'm not a V

Let me see, how can you prove it to me?

Short of me fucking your brains out idk what would suffice

Do you eat pussy?

Yes, like not all the time but sometimes

Ok weird answer

I mean I don't just walk around offering those services

Where is the G spot?

C'mon are we really going to go there?

Where is there?

It's a mysterious pleasure zone deep within the vaginal cavity

That sounds sorta medical - but close enough

What do you mean?

It's not "deep" within, just an inch or so and on the top wall

If we are gonna talk sex lets at least make it sexy so I have something to work w later

When you are receiving head, do you like lots of hand action, mouth action, spitting, gagging, all of the above or none of the above?

Loaded question, I suppose I would like to answer that I like it sensual

Ok and is it easier for you to cum w the girl doing reverse cowgirl or simple doggy style?

Is this a trick question?

No, think on it

[The 39-year-old woman of Iranian descent who police say opened fire at YouTube's California headquarters was an animal rights defender and vegan vlogger who was upset with the video-sharing website for demonetizing her videos. Some of her videos included vegan-cooking tutorials, workouts, parody music videos, and disturbing images and videos of animal abuse]

[incel: aka involuntarily celibate, a person (usually male) who has a horrible personality and treats women like sexual objects and thinks his lack of a sex life comes from being "ugly" when it's really his blatant sexism and terrible attitude. Incels have little to no self awareness; even when they see other "ugly" men with girlfriends, they consider these men to be tricksters who have somehow beat the system and can get women despite being cursed with unattractiveness (in other words, they're respectful to women and women are attracted to their personalities, but incels can't comprehend such a phenomenon). They believe that women owe them sex, and many of the more extreme incels like to spend time in incel communities on the internet coming up with ways to make women have sex with them (often involving genocide of people of color, genocide of "Chads" (men who have sex), taking rights away from women, raping them, having sex with women's dead bodies, and other horrid, disgusting things]

[megalomania: delusion about one's own power or importance, typically as a symptom of manic or paranoid disorder]

[deflection: an intense focus upon and antagonism toward the legitimacy of the actions, feelings, and beliefs of others, especially the partner, and an intense misdirection of attention away from the primary aggressor's actions]

[The G-spot lies on the anterior wall of the vagina, about 5-8cm above the opening to the vagina. It is easiest to locate if a woman lies on her back and has someone else insert one or two fingers into the vagina with the palm up]

[Reverse Cowgirl: The man lies on his back, legs are straight, slightly driven apart, and his head is raised. The woman sits on top of the male partner back to him, her legs are bent in the knees and her feet are stretched out along the body of the male partner. With one hand she holds the man's knee, while he puts one hand on the woman's waist and with the second one he fondles her breast, or some variation]

DAY•NINETEEN

Doggy style

So you had all night to think about it, did you look it up?

No, doggy is my jam

Ok that is the correct answer

What do I win?

I won't call you an incel anymore

Deal

What's the latest hot virus talk?

It's all over the place, what category do you want? Cultural, science, obscene, funny dept

Science for 1000

Well there is word that the original models out of England, the ones that were the basis for the millions of projected deaths, may have been wrong, very wrong

And is this official yet?

It's official if you believe certain doctors and scientists, but not if you follow the lead of particular politicians

It does seem political at this point

Politicians have taken over and now it's not so much about hospital rooms but about us staying lockdown indefinitely

Like I said, keep an eye on what we are not supposed to be seeing

The conspiracy world is quite abuzz

As they should be

[that's my jam: Using the term my jam has superseded simply being relevant to a specific song that is your favorite, it is now relevant to any specific subject matter. It can be used to describe any one thing that you feel you enjoy more than the majority of other options in the same category]

[Imperial College Infectious Disease Model: Two fundamental strategies are possible: (a) mitigation, which focuses on slowing but not necessarily stopping epidemic spread, while reducing peak healthcare demand along with protecting those most at risk of severe disease from infection, and (b) suppression, which aims to reverse epidemic growth, reducing case numbers to low levels and maintaining that situation indefinitely]

DAY•TWENTY

Do you ever wonder what I sound like?

No, sorry but it hasn't crossed my mind

It's okay no offense taken

I know enough about you from what you have shared

From that can you deduce what my voice is like?

Yes, I have a good idea of everything I need to know about you

I feel that about you too but I would like a pic

You men are visual animals

Yes we are

Can't you allow the theater of your mind to construct how I look?

I can fantasize all day and night but what if I am totally wrong?

Like you're beating off to someone that looks nothing like me?

Yes

And that yoga ass that you obsess over may not be what you thought it was

Well

Maybe there are aspects of my physical self that would disgust you

I doubt that, you see I deal well w your attitude

You mean my snarkiness

I guess you could call it that

Or my certain dead in inside ness

Do you feel that way?

Partially yes, there are numbed out areas of my totality

And why is that?

Self-preservation I suppose - you go through some shit, you put up some walls and then those walls stay up

And here you are projecting this onto me, making me feel bad about myself

Oh hell I am not, if you feel that way then bye boy

• • •

Hey, I didn't mean what I said earlier, about projecting

It's all good, I am probably doing some of that

I enjoy our talks, even if we are not meeting up anytime soon

Soon? Like ever?

Let's not go there

Look, I like you, so far you seem to be a nice person, just slightly off track, but if I compare you to most ppl you are a gem

I am not fully myself with all that's going on

I get it, who really is anymore

Methinks when this is all over we will all be a bit stronger, with a smaller threshold for bullshit

"Methinks" are you some incel lord now?

Damn autocorrect

Those that do survive, and don't break under the pressure and do something rash

I am hearing calls to suicide lines are up, like tenfold

Imagine the pressure of having a family to support and you're out a job w no timelines for return

What surprises me is how little savings ppl have

Why? It's about choices

Like the avg family has only a few hundred dollars

Maybe they like living on the edge, maybe it's a rush for them, maybe they don't understand personal responsibility, maybe it's nothing more than an adverse relationship w money

Like those 911 widows who blew through their blood money insurance payouts

Some of that psychology, but more like they were never raised w a healthy money relationship

It's not something we learn in school, so you gotta learn it at home

And that's the problem, you grow up seeing the struggle, a parent flustered by his/her incompetence to provide, and money now becomes this evil thing that is so elusive

But they are not too far off w that

Or the alternative is you accept money as something that can provide you freedoms, that money comes to you frequently, and in abundance

Sounds New Agey

It's basic laws of attraction

I'm glad you have it figured out

I'm not even going to ask you what you do

Well, it's complicated

Not asking, so don't divulge - good night

[snarkiness: Origin of snarky, from dialectal snark to nag from
snark, snork to snore, snort from Dutch and Low German
snorken of imitative origin; (informal) snide and sarcastic;
usually out of irritation, often humorously]

[self-preservation: behavior based on the characteristics or
feelings that warn people or animals to protect themselves
from difficulties or dangers]

[methinks: archaic: it seems to me; Middle English me thinketh, from Old English mē thincth, from mē (dative of ic I) + thincth seems, from thyncan to seem]

[9/11 Widows: Those who took the $7 million each, described by many as blood money, were banned from suing the government or airlines for further compensation, and future rights were stripped away. Those who willingly accepted the compensation also found that it brought little solace. Kathy Trant made national headlines when her spending spree turned her into a celebrity. An attractive blonde, she spent $5 million rather quickly, wanting to quickly disperse of the funds as there was a 'disturbing association' tied to the money. Her purchases included half a million on designer shoes, five figures on Botox injections, and matching breast enlargement surgeries for her and her Long Island girlfriends]

DAY•TWENTY ONE

How much at risk do you think society is at this point?

What a sentence

Complicated?

No I just feel like I had a mini stroke reading it

Sorry

Don't apologize

So your thoughts?

If we survive then yeah it's gonna be different

How so?

In every single way, but most importantly how ppl get back to interaction

I'm tired of the isolation

Look, we need each other, it's getting old

I'm not that social to begin with but now I want to make more friends

I could use losing some friends at this point, and I'm sure I will

I miss simple things like a nice barista or a nodding smile from a stranger

What about sex? Oh that's right, you're an incel

Ouch, take that back

I kid. It's gonna take time but I think we go back to normal

By then there will be a second wave

What's that?

A new outbreak of a stronger strain, in the fall when the weather cools down

Oh hell no

Yes, it seems like it's almost certain at this point

But how can they predict that?

All the top doctors and scientists are saying it

Aren't these the same ones that keep getting everything wrong?

Some yes

And what about opposing viewpoints?

Those are being debunked

Didn't I tell you to lay off the fear porn?

I'm just trying to stay informed

The news is no longer information, it's emotions and feelings

I wonder how all this debunking is taking place, so fast, like right after something is published it gets killed off - even regular ppl online are becoming experts and shooting down medical info

You mean the sheeple?

Is that what you call them?

It's easier that way. I just throw them all into that and it makes it easier to discern the madness

My problem is gauging who is gullible versus who may be correct

Like some burnout dude you know online is now an epidemiologist disease expert? It's not that hard

You're right but sometimes it's the conviction they have, that delivery is what is so convincing

Just cuz someone is nuts and adamant about their doubled down stance doesn't mean you need to follow them over the edge

I'm not saying that, I get it that there are multiple groups that could be wrong, it's just difficult to get past the conviction

Then join a cult

Why?

Or an MLM

MLM?

Multi level marketing scheme where the sheeple graze

Like Herbalife?

Yes, and there are many more, that was one of the originals

My uncle sold it and drove the entire family away, apparently he pulled them all in and every single one got burned

Yes, so it's like that, groupthink, suspension of logic in the pursuit of something easy - same for the virus, it's easier to default to the victim setting, to roll over and take the punches, to rely on govt handouts, to be scared to return to work, to give in and gain some weight, to justify it w end of world apocalyptic thinking

Wow that's deep

No it's not, and if you really think that then you should join the sheep

[second wave: a phenomenon of infections that can develop during a pandemic. The disease infects one group of people first, then as infections appear to decrease new infections increase in a different part of the population, resulting in a second wave of infections]

[debunked: to expose the falseness or hollowness of a myth, idea, or belief]

[fear porn: Content that is fear-based and often about the end of the world in some way. Highly addictive for its paranoia and dissociation side effects tied to the existential threat within the narrative]

[sheeple: people compared to sheep in being docile, foolish, or easily led]

[Multi Level Marketing Cult Theory: Network marketing businesses are based not on reality but on a buy-in of what could be. They operate like a religion in that they have an answer for everything where all success comes from proper behavior and all failure stems from an individual shortcoming. Often faith based organizations with no room to question and little tolerance for true creativity, they need and demand obedience]

[groupthink: the practice of thinking or making decisions as a group in a way that discourages creativity or individual responsibility]

DAY•TWENTY TWO

Apparently I may sound paranoid or sheep-like to say this but it's not like the flu, it's much worse, more fatal and way more contagious

Well good morning to you

I just want you to know where I'm coming from

I get it but am I supposed to agree with you? Am I allowed to have my own thoughts and come to my own conclusions?

Yes I just want you to know what we are dealing with

Is this from your trusted news sources?

Yes, and other research

Any counter narratives out there to debunk?

I guess, like for anything

So basically you woke me up to scare me with your new findings?

Sorry if I woke you

Of all the things we can talk about in the history of humanity it's more hot virus talk?

Well it is what's on everyone's minds

Not mine

What's on yours?

Anything but that - my yoga class, a good book, the taste of a new merlot on my tongue, the pleasure of a hot bath

I'm happy for you

Why is that?

That you can suspend your fear and go to the pleasurable things

There is no fear to suspend - I don't possess it

It must be nice to not have it to begin with

Boy you are losing points w me today

Sorry but I don't get your cavalier attitude

What's so cavalier about it, I don't believe the hype

I guess that's what makes us different

Um you think, that and lots more

• • •

All of this has me wondering if we should appreciate more regular life, without all the disruptions, or if we are even going back to that

So you mean like less folks complaining about shit?

That and a sense of gratitude for a simplified existence

I been living that dream for years - keep it simple stupid

I guess it's an entire couple of generations that have not seen any real adversity and settled into a rat race mentality, not for material possessions but who could outdo one another w looks, or experiences - the whole digital fortress we live in

Social media?

Yes keeping up w the Joneses and pleasing your own audience, however false that sense of security is

Wow, boo I am proud of these newfound thoughts

It's a bunch of self aggrandizing, with the only real satisfied recipient being yourself

That's why I don't do it, never have and never will

And I think it's making these kids brain dead, like blowing out the dopamine receptors

It comes down to the analog versus the digital

And they take that seeking out of analog experiences for their digital portfolio, it's sick really - how about just go a day without your phone and take in some nature

Do you think the virus will cause a digital reckoning?

I hope so, something needs to break it

But I always hear ppl keep coming back because of our fear of missing out

It does get alluring, drawing you back in

What if you reframed your mindset to a joy of missing out?

Like you get off through not knowing?

Yes exactly, and the same for news

Wouldn't that be something

[Keep it simple, stupid (KISS) is a design principle which states that designs and/or systems should be as simple as possible. Wherever possible, complexity should be avoided in a system—as simplicity guarantees the greatest levels of user acceptance and interaction]

[rat race: an endless, self-defeating, or pointless pursuit, with the phrase equating humans to rats attempting to earn a reward such as cheese, in vain. It may also refer to a competitive struggle to get ahead financially or routinely. The term is commonly associated with an exhausting, repetitive lifestyle that leaves no time for relaxation or enjoyment]

[analog versus digital: analog experiences are, at their core, more hands-on, personalized experiences, while digital experiences are often designed through feedback and are limited to less possibilities of serendipitous connections]

[FOMO: fear of missing out; an anxiety brought about by an exciting or interesting event which may currently be happening elsewhere, often aroused by posts seen on social media]

[JOMO: joy of missing out; a feeling of contentment with one's own pursuits and activities, without worrying over the possibility of missing out on what others may be doing]

DAY•TWENTY THREE

Good morning

Did you sleep well?

Not much, thinking about this 'new normal'

I wouldn't call it normal

This disruption of events becoming normal life

Like black swan events?

What's that?

Something beyond 'any expectations w severe consequences'

Yes certainly it's looking like that now

Is that what the news says?

I don't know how you can deny how bad it is out there

I'm not but I'm unplugged from it

I don't know how you do that

I worry only about my immediate circumstance and environment - it's quite simple

But not knowing what's swirling around us is kinda irresponsible

Not for me, I'm quite content with my life on a micro level

Does this ever make you feel selfish?

Honey boo you need to understand something, your own feelings are more important than those of others - as selfish as that sounds that is how mental wellness works

But I can't help but think of all the suffering

That's sweet but you need to focus on yourself and not be so goddamn scared

I do obsess over these things

Honestly it's unattractive

Oh yeah?

Yeah, I bet you did anything and everything to please your overbearing mother, amirite?

How did you know?

You are an adult product of that environment and now as a grown up it's keeping you from advancing - like your obsession w the fear mongering

Sorry but it seems you are not taking this seriously enough

Life is too serious to be taken seriously

Wow

Let that sink in

I guess it would be better if I dialed back my worried nature

Yeah you are doing no one any favors especially yourself, and if you want to meet up in RL after this your chances are dimming

Okay roger that

• • •

If you find gratitude in the day to day you find slivers of wisdom

You're back?

And with wisdom comes a certain level of peace

Umkay

This is what some call nirvana

The band?

And this is what I'm chasing, and it's not hard to get there really - just being grateful for the small things, warmth, clothes, meals, entertainment

I guess we are conditioned for more than that, like constantly seeking out the unattainable

Bingo, the unattainable - think about that, it's like chasing a carrot that is constantly moving ahead of you

I see lots of stuff online that kinda pisses me off

What did I tell you about the online world?

I know I'm trying to pull it back

What's your observation?

Just that there is a collective coolness, this vibe that it's all good, beautiful people w their lives fully figured out, then there are regulars, normies, like us, that could never get there no matter what we did

Like you're missing the talent or the money?

Yes, there is that, and the luck. So much goes into how they got there, for everyone else it really is just unattainable - yet we mimic

That's what society does best

I see shit like the resurgence of the workout clothes like Champion, and I'm like that is some ghetto wear for the poor kids, my mom used to buy me that when I was a kid for like $2 a shirt

Now it's blowing up

Yes, so I'm like wtf is going on? Come to find out some reality show family started wearing it - and not by accident, they got paid like a million

So you are seeing that much of how we are supposed to believe is coming off a script

It's scary

So remember that next time you freak out by what you see on the news

That reminds me, I wanted to tell you something funny

What's that?

You know how this virus isn't affecting children for whatever reason, well now there is a push to get them back into school, cuz basically nobody can go to work if their kids are home

Yes, and nobody is gonna learn from a day drunk mom

Exactly, so now the news is pushing a new pediatric disease. Wait for it, completely unrelated to the virus but suddenly super fatal for children

Not surprised

Yeah and I looked it up and this has been around forever and has super low mortality rates

[black swan event: an unpredictable event that is beyond what is normally expected of a situation and has potentially severe consequences, characterized by their extreme rarity, their severe impact, and widespread insistence, black swan events are often obvious in hindsight]

[amirite: short for 'am I right?']

[nirvana: a transcendent state in which there is neither suffering, desire, nor sense of self, and the subject is released from the effects of karma and the cycle of death and rebirth. It represents the final goal of Buddhism]

DAY•TWENTY FOUR

Remember how yesterday I was saying how we are just trying to keep up with those we see online

Yeah

The psychology behind it is giving kids anxiety. When I say kids I mean adults. The constant ideal being thrust down their throats isn't allowing them any time to breathe

It's by design my friend

It's leading to them avoiding going into public, it even gets them to avoid speaking to others as a way to avoid stumbling when they speak

Wow

And the whole eye contact thing, forget about it - any sense of awkward moments are squashed with the ability to pull out your phone and look busy

I grew up facing awkward moments and looking someone in the eyes, that was healthy

So it leads to a crippling anxiety, something nobody can squelch

And this is why we have safe spaces

Pretty much

Yeah when you have easily triggered adults ready to go off at any moment you need places for them to chill out LOL

What if this whole virus thing is nothing more than the entire world being swallowed into one big safe space?

Ha lol

No for real, like the fear culture has won, the news narrative has won, enough of a majority are scared into lockdown submission

You may be onto something

We never stopped to think how fast this all went down

And without any questions

And zero rebellion

It was like let's see how much we can get away with

And the ppl just went along with it

That idea that millions would die

That you were selfish if you didn't comply

The peer pressure lol

And we need the hospitals to be ready to take the victims

And your role is crucial

Social distance is all we ask

Your forefathers fought on the beaches of Normandy while your contribution is comfy athleisure and binge-worthy television

And don't forget the take out food

Lest we forget unlimited porn

There is that

It helps fight rebellion they say, like conjugal visits from the old lady

Ok whatever

Now I'm thinking how do we get back

Back to how it was?

Yes, the reboot

It may not look the same

[snowflake theory: today's youth have been coddled by helicopter parents and allowed to avoid the responsibility and independence that foster mental resilience, combined with heavy social media usage that works against developmental goals, including physical, cognitive, relations, sexual and maturational]

[safe spaces: places created for individuals who feel marginalized to come together to communicate regarding their experiences with marginalization, most commonly located on university campuses, but also at workplaces]

[conjugal visit: a scheduled period in which an inmate of a prison or jail is permitted to spend several hours in private with a visitor, usually their legal spouse. The parties may engage in sexual activity]

DAY●TWENTY FIVE

What is your idealized post-virus world?

Less ppl on the streets

Less cars would be good

Can you see how clear the sky is now?

It's amazing, it's like the sun is brighter and the plants are all greener

Maybe less idol worship

That would be nice, it seems to be underway

No sports and we don't hear from the athletes

Nor the rich actors in their mansions complaining about lockdown

Save me the lectures y'all

Something that's always got me tripping is the advice that celebrities like to dish out - as if they are all knowing, like we even asked for it

Yeah it's got to be taken with a grain of salt

Or not taken at all

Or that

Look at Oprah for example, that woman gives advice all day long, she is the messiah for so many, yet she dishes wisdom on losing weight but she is fat, or relationship advice yet she has never been married, advice on parenting, no kids, so on

Good point, we should be taking the lead from those w actual experience

Yeah and that could be some rando in your life, it doesnt have to be a new sensation that has been famous for a minute, or some closeted lesbian like Oprah

Closeted lez?

Well that has been the word for years, her male companion is just a beard

A beard?

A cover story for a down low gay

Gotcha, then her friend Gayle is it, she must be her real lover

Yes

[for every 30 days of lockdown there are significantly reduced road traffic and industrial emissions, and a lowering of nitrogen dioxide levels, also known as PM2.5, which result in 1.3 million fewer days of work absence, 6,000 fewer children developing asthma, 1,900 avoided emergency room visits and 600 fewer premature births]

[Oprah and Gayle King have enjoyed a long personal and professional relationship spanning over 40 years, from their days working at a Baltimore TV station, to becoming media moguls and world-renowned personalities. Oprah officially set the record straight in the most telling interview of her career, speaking to Barbara Walters to discuss the ending of her famed talk-show. The fact that the question was featured at all shows how prevalent of a rumour it was. Breaking into tears, she shared: "Why would you want to hide it? She's the mother I never had. She's the sister everybody would want. She's the friend everybody deserves. I don't know a better person." The prevalence of down low culture within the black community, especially black celebrities, is a result of their community in general not allowing for open gay sexuality, so because of this stigma the Oprah rumors will likely remain status quo]

DAY•TWENTY SIX

How do you feel about your body?

Is this a trap?

No I was reading about male satisfaction with offline peer groups versus social media posts

And nothing about women?

No this is about men, women's body issues have been around forever. And so they asked these men to choose from a stack of different male body types, silhouettes of male bodies in a line, starting w obese to ultra buffed out

And then?

The majority chose their ideal to be two levels hotter than wherever they were at - so a really fat dude went for the dad bod and the dad bods went for the bodybuilder look

Interesting

What the test revealed is that nobody chose their actual own body type

I wonder what women would do

The same thing or maybe even worse

I've heard some women like dad bods

Yes nothing wrong with it at all - being a dad or not, just that real body is a turn on

I think the same for women, I don't even mind chubby girls

Then you're not gonna like me, chubby chaser

I dont mean chubby like morbidly obese, just saying some meat on the bones, cushion for the pushin

Well there is lots of that out there

People are joking about how much weight everyone is gonna gain during this

Not me, I'm actually down a couple pounds

Pics or it didnt happen

[chubby chasers: anyone attracted to fat people, whether the person is male, female, gay or straight doesn't come into it]

[pics or it didn't happen: a phrase used on internet forums to counter the vast range of unverifiable claims made by users. Often these claims involve personal brag-worthy accomplishments, extraordinary or rare sights/occurrences, and tales relating to alcohol or drug use]

DAY•TWENTY SEVEN

I read that having a perceived sense of knowledge helps in emotional well-being

Does this explain all the experts among us?

Yes, if you can somehow craft a narrative that you know something others don't know

And then dogmatically preach it

That would be one's own reinforcement of the ideas

Like they are fooling themselves to feel safer?

Yes something of a false shell and then when it gets questioned a move into the doubling down phase

There is some of that going on now around us

Exactly, oh wait, I thought you weren't watching the news

I'm not but it's in the ether, lets say

And in this doubling down the story often gets further shredded, and the original fervent stance is more and more debunked, leading to the emperor has no clothes effect

It will be interesting when the dust settles who was right and who was wrong

More likely it will be washed away and we will move our attention, or rather our attention will deliberately be directed elsewhere, and there will be no accountability

Well said boo

Even with all of these masks there is an unmasking taking place

It's like we are in some bad sci fi movie and they are figuring out the plot as we go

I was thinking it was a well-orchestrated master plan but now it seems to be playing out organically, and the two sides are more and more predictable

Two sides?

Pretty much the believers and the non-believers

There are those who don't believe it's real, no?

It's real for everyone but the numbers, the actual human carnage versus the projections, then those who are all in on lockdown, on paranoia, on not having to go to work, and most alarmingly those who willingly go with what the govt tells them

I think we are going to hit a boiling point and it will begin to settle down

And then the accusations and new effort at rebuild

If there are enough that want that

True

There are ppl who like destruction and demise, those who want to see shit crashing down around them

Those sick fucks lol

Some of it is that but it could be their mentality towards the world, like they were abused kids, or they don't own anything so they don't know what it's like to build something up and maintain it

I don't own much but I'm not like that

Not you boo, you get it - we need more ppl like you

It would be a better place wouldn't it

But then I would have to share you

As long as you find me a girlfriend, or a friend w benefits

Oh hell no I'm not going to that extreme, I want you all to myself

Then send nudes to hold me over

Brazen...I like it

Less talking and more doing

[emperor has no clothes: an expression used to describe a situation in which people are afraid to criticize something or someone because the perceived wisdom of the masses is that the thing or person is good or important]

[current generational trend is to opt out of accumulating stuff and instead to explore experiences with conventional markers of success; like what you own no longer is meaningful; all the while a disillusionment with the status quo has removed much of previous limits on life choices]

[send nudes: Not all nude photographs are created equal, and not all pictures highlight the same body parts. Roughly a quarter of nudes show the face, while breasts, chests, and nipples are the most popular subject, particularly with women. Half of men will send genitalia shots, with one in five sending full body with face nudes]

DAY•TWENTY EIGHT

Don't update your phone's software if you don't need to

Why is that? Good morning btw

The new versions are allowing tracer software plug-ins

Plug-ins?

It's updates that can trace those who have the virus and where they travel, and where you travel and who comes into contact with you

Sounds complicated, like does it test you?

No but somehow the main database knows who has the virus and when you download the update it gives permission to access all of your contacts and then it collects info on all of them

So it sounds like the software works like a virus lol

Yes, so in theory we are all going to get pulled into it anyway

Well lets see, in the last month I have only left my apartment a handful of times and that was within a couple blocks to buy groceries, wine, a new yoga mat, and tampons

Do tell

Ok Prince Charles

What does that mean?

Prince Charles and his gf years ago got busted talking on the phone about him wanting to be her tampon

Omg

It was called Tampongate, super embarrassing for the royal family

It's just when you mention tampon my mind goes to your crotch

Is that so, and without any clues, what image do you create of my crotch?

I guess it's a composite crotch

Umkay

It's a collective bended image of a nicely shaped subtle cameltoe situated in thick yoga pants

Why thick?

Like padded, like aligning your thighs with the flat lower belly over the lady parts

That's sweet, I have a flat tummy

It's easy to figure that out about you, your fitness regimen and penchant for wine makes me think you don't eat much and when you do it's clean, and your metabolism takes care of the empty calories from the wine

And my cameltoe?

It's nothing but a placeholder in the erotic makeup of you as the whole

Like something defining about me?

Yes, a striking reminder that under the stretch polyester there is a vagina, a slit, a series of labia and ultimately a hole

Ok obgyn

This opposed to a man's package, it's all about the opposing qualities

I thought men were more into ass

Yes we are, those who dial in on the cameltoe seem to be more of fetishists

Ass I have heard is a turn-on because it symbolizes fertility

There is that, and some plumpness is more attractive than rail thin and boney

A dude in our yoga class I think is there solely for all the bending ass, he is always in the back row and doesn't do all the poses - I keep thinking the teacher is going to kick him out but he is there every week

He is probably hard as a rock

Yeah the girls, about ten of us are in 2 rows of like 5 and when we get on all fours and flare out our lower backs, that is full ass spread

And he is just sitting there taking it in?

I tend to look back at him and he has this glazed over look like he is trying to follow the teacher and is having to look up at the front even though he is staring right into someone's butthole

Creepers are gonna creep

I think some of the girls like it - it's not like he is attractive at all but he is fit and that by itself can be a turn on

There is probably an entire genre of porn for that

What yoga sex?

Yes like an instructor stretching out his students then slipping them a digit, next thing you know the pants are down and they are shagging

I'm sure you're right - not that I watch much porn but I'm partial to the real estate porn

Like pictures of nice big houses?

No, like porns that take place during an open house, a buyer shows up to see the house and the realtor fucks them

Oh my, I need to look that up

It's late, night night

[Contact tracing software can be an important tool in the public health's arsenal to gain a holistic picture of the pandemic and tamp down on disease spread, especially when public spaces and businesses eventually reopen. The capability relies on an application programming interface letting approved tracing apps tap into a smartphone's Bluetooth radio and monitor whether the user is close to someone who is infected or later tests positive]

[Tampongate (AKA Camillagate) was a scandal that unfolded in 1993, when the transcript of a phone call between Prince Charles and his then-mistress, Camilla Parker-Bowles, was published in the press. The racy, six-minute phone call reportedly took place in 1989, when Charles was still married to Princess Diana, and Camilla was still married to Andrew Parker Bowles, and it included an overwhelmingly horny exchange about Charles yearning to be a feminine hygiene product. CHARLES: "Oh, God, I'll just live inside your trousers or something. It would be much easier!" CAMILLA: "What are you going to turn into, a pair of knickers? CHARLES: "Or God forbid a Tampax. Just my luck." CAMILLA: "You are a complete idiot! Oh what a wonderful idea." CHARLES: "My luck to be chucked down a lavatory and go on and on forever swirling round on the top, never going down."

[camel toe, or cameltoe, is slang for the outline of a woman's labia majora in tightly fitting clothes. Owing to a combination of anatomical factors and the tightness of the fabric covering the area, the crotch and mons pubis may display a shape resembling the forefoot of a camel. Camel toe commonly occurs as a result of wearing tight-fitting clothes, such as leggings, shorts, hot pants or swimwear]

DAY•TWENTY NINE

Fear fatigue is setting in

Your own or others?

Both I guess, just seeing it everywhere without the massive risk to justify it

Like this virus is fake?

No like it's not as dangerous as everyone is led to believe and that somehow nobody is talking about that

Fear sells

I know it's healthy to have a sense of fear, it's our reptilian brain engaging and looking out for danger

But it's looking for it in nature

Exactly, not manufactured by a 'news' crew off of a narrative spoon fed to them from above

And this fear is leading to other things that will come at us later, like a collapsed economy

It isn't all about money but I know what you're saying

The economy isn't just Wall Street and corporate bottom lines, it is how all of this works, it's the blood of the system

Umkay professor

I'm just saying that if and when this virus is gone or dealt with we will have so much more to deal with

A post-virus world will look different but it may be for the better

Shed some of the unnecessary aspects

Too much commuting

Reusable grocery bags, gross

Movie theaters

Concerts

No!

Porn sets, orgies

Now you're talking

You see, it does sound too preposterous

Yeah like when you think it through the only logical return is to exactly what we had

Creatures of comfort, it's what we do best

And those who want change can stay home

Yes if they choose to remain afraid, by all means do not leave your safe space

I imagine the day it lifts there being a glorious moment right out of a movie, everyone walking out of their front doors squinting into the bright glare of the sun, w birds chirping and all

Dont forget all the ppl that will want to hook up - lots of sex that day

And the gullible schmucks who choose fear over fact will just be denying themselves for the sake of a virtue signal

[virtue signalling is to take a conspicuous but essentially useless action ostensibly to support a good cause but actually to show off how much more moral you are than everybody else by posting it on social media or sharing with those within your immediate reach]

DAY•THIRTY

Instead of forever alone now it's more like together alone

That must be comforting for them

Who is "them"?

Those who need catchphrases to find solace for their sad and empty existence

Ouch

Not ouch, I'm just calling out the bullshit of how some ppl need to encapsulate everything they do into a feel good mantra

Well, good morning

If it feels good so be it, but there is danger in acquiescing your legitimate concerns and fears to a well-designed feel good sequence of words. I get it, it's really just the damaged ppl who need it, and in their own sanctimony they feel like they need to bring everyone else in on it

Like virtue signaling?

Bingo

And feelings over facts

Yes, simply put, going about life looking for trouble, seeking out outrage, anything to get the ppl talking and to elevate themselves onto a pedestal of righteousness. However false that stage may be doesn't matter because it's all about optics

Well put, this does seem to be the new wave of politics overtaking culture

Culture? What culture is left? It's all about being offended, haven't you noticed?

This statement offends me

And when it is all outrage all the time there is no room for self growth or advancement of any kind

I'm trying to keep it real

I'm not talking about you, and don't take everything so personally

Sorry

Within this there is solidarity toward a single cause, the emotional response, or disgust of something - like political divides, or in this case those who are all in on the virus scare or those who think it's nothing more than a hoax

A hoax for what?

For whatever purpose, it doesn't matter - if I had to guess, to destabilize the global model, to crash economies, to instill fear that will have long term consequences on the economy

Interesting

And to go along with it, for the long haul ride, and to not question the authorities, is to lay down a path forward that won't require a fight, just a full succumbing to whatever is decided for you

Like giving in?

Yes on a large scale, we are at this tipping point now

Like irrevocable change?

Yes if it hits critical mass there could be a shift in this nation's deocratic structure

With as many flaws I think we have let's hope that doesn't happen

You see there is a political elite in America, it's finally coming out

But you have to look for it

It's right there in front of us, just analyze what's going on

And those politicians don't want to lose any power

Exactly, they don't want that and they don't want anyone investigating how it was possible that they became so rich - so they hide behind worker rights, fighting for the struggling families, while they live w govt protection, and their family members profit off of their access

I am seeing some big names getting nervous

Yeah look closely to how they speak, something is up, their passions and concerns are not normal political differences - they are hiding something and all we can hope is that it comes out

[outrage culture consists of calling someone out online, sometimes referred to as call-out culture, it's a form of public humiliation or shaming that aims to hold individuals and groups accountable for actions perceived to be offensive by other individuals or groups, who then call attention to this behavior, usually on social media]

[critical mass explained in scientific terms: when a nuclear chain reaction in a mass of fissile material is self-sustaining, the mass is said to be in a critical state in which there is no increase or decrease in power, temperature, or neutron population, and when k = 1, the mass becomes critical, and the chain reaction becomes self-sustaining]

[In political and sociological theory, the elite (French élite, from Latin eligere, to select or to sort out) are a small group of powerful people who hold a disproportionate amount of wealth, privilege, political power, or skill in a society]

DAY•THIRTY ONE

"Connected solitude" - so hot right now

What's that?

Just something I read from a Health Director who said it may still be months before the lockdown ends

I can't imagine it going on that long

I can, it's all about controlling the ppl and the agenda now is clear, that some ppl want to destroy the economy

But I thought it was about flattening the curve

Oh did you miss that news, it was flattened last week

So now what's it about?

Choose your poison, second wave? Kids may get it? Schools need to stay closed? It's more deadly than we thought? A vaccine?

At some point the ppl will rise up

You would hope but not when there is social shaming into thinking you are being selfish by putting others at risk with your questions of authority lol

Lol that does seem to be the trend

• • •

Where did you go?

My phone died, and you know what? I let it die

Our convos are that interesting?

No not because of you boo, just because I wanted to see it shut itself down

Oh

Into its own hibernation w me disconnected from the outside world, and a forced break while it recharges

I should try that some time but I have this huge charger collection so it would need to be deliberate

Try it, you may like it - when it went off I was able to stretch my neck and exercise my wrists

Do tell

Small yoga moves to fight the cradle neck and carpal tunnel that come from heavy cell usage

I feel like an old man sometimes

There is going to be an entire generation fucked up by cell phones, not to mention eyesight in relation to the screen

And all of the ambient noise

Easy access to gaming and porn

That too

It's like you kids don't really need to seek things out in the real world

Who you calling kid?

Your phones are mobile morphine drip devices

I do consciously take breaks

Yeah right, you don't need to lie to me

I mean I will set it down if I'm cooking or showering

But the rest of the time it's in your hand

Pretty much but that's just how it is now

Sure but it's not healthy, it will be a while but it will finally come out

Come out?

How unhealthy they are. This happened with cigarettes. Doctors used to smoke and tell patients to smoke, for a while in the 50s everyone was lighting it up, with the idea that it was good for you. Housewives loved it cuz it kept the weight off. But then forty years on there were some whistleblowers within the industry that dropped the dime, exposing how dangerous cigarettes were. It's gonna happen w phones

So put porn and gaming into that category

Yes, look around you - not now in your apartment or mommy's house, but at this generation - blown out minds, limp dicks, chasing dopamine in loop feeding cycles

So how does it end?

It begins w the so called incels, much of their lack of drive is a result of it - then it ends w insecurity on a massive scale, some of that already is in play in the collective fear brigade pathos of succumbing to whatever daddy govt says

That's deep I kinda lost you

If it's inherent within us to compare ourselves to others, it now becomes heightened with devices that spread the comparing, to then find yourself as inadequate in comparison to all the beauty around you, or all the sex ppl are having, or the comforts of a made life. Then there is you there questioning your own self, that flabby tummy or empty bank account. In that despair you are challenged with rising up, from nothing, at a deficit even...or going w the govt narrative and being a good citizen who will collectively get through this

That's deep

Do you follow?

Roger, copy

It's easier to give in, especially when the govt is giving you a road map - and when you are also too dumb to realize the govt doesnt have your best interest at heart

I did think something along those lines when they allowed the liquor stores to stay open but churches closed

Thank you

For what?

For seeing through the fog machine of distortion

It's like booze and religion are similar devices, but the consumers are who are different, and one is taxed

I am impressed w your analysis

So you keep the drunkards happy cuz we all know a few drinks will calm the nerves, while some right-leaning church goer, probably someone who doesn't even drink, is denied their chance to worship in a church, to congregate and be fed a sermon

How did you get so smart boo? Am I finally rubbing off on you?

I read that last text as 'rubbing on you' but a boy can dream

[connected solitude does not have the same negative connotations that are attached to loneliness, as loneliness is characterized by a subjective negative feeling that we can be surrounded by others but still feel lonely, while solitude is a state of being away from society]

DAY•THIRTY TWO

Hey good morning

• • •

Hope you're ok, just saying hello

• • •

Well good night, hope your phone is dead, and everything is ok

DAY•THIRTY THREE

Good morning

• • •

I hope I didn't say something to piss you off. I looked back at our message for a clue. I didn't see anything, just hoping you are okay. Please don't ghost me

• • •

To be totally honest. I need our talks, I look forward to nothing more than to hear from you

• • •

Well good night, please just let me know you are okay xoxo

[Ghosting is a colloquial term used to describe the practice of ceasing all communication and contact with a partner, friend, or similar individual without any apparent warning or justification and subsequently ignoring any attempts to reach out or communications made by said partner, friend, or individual]

DAY•THIRTY FOUR

You there?

Yes, thank god you are alive

Why did you panic so hard, it's not really a good look to be honest

Idk I was afraid you were hurt or something, then it set in maybe you were disconnecting from me

Conscious uncoupling?

I guess, I just really felt lost

Well, I had company but they are gone now

What do you mean you had company?

Exactly that, am I not allowed that?

Well, what about the quarantine? Are you trying to get killed?

A lady has needs, and sometimes those needs get satisfied

You mean you had sex, a gigolo come over? I can't believe this conversation

You seem pissed, should we have this talk another time?

No I'm not pissed just a little jealous, and would like to know what happened

An old flame came by, we had sex and he slept over and now he is gone

Wow just wow

I'm sorry but you are not my bf or husband

I have no words right now

● ● ●

Let me get this straight, this guy just came over and you hooked up?

Yes pretty much

Did you use protection?

I wore a mask

WTF

No, I know he is clean, like I said we used to date so we did this before - it's like friends w benefits

You could have waited for me

I don't even know what you look like - this guy I know him - don't trip he doesn't even live here

So he drove to your place, illegally, breaking all these laws for some pussy?

That's what some men will do, and in a way it's a turn on

Okay now this convo is getting weird

We all have needs, and it becomes a calculation with fear versus desire

You never told me about this guy before

Why would I, there have been lots of exes

"Lots" - define lots

Like total number of boyfriends or total number of guys I've hooked up with?

I would hope that number is the same

No, child, the hook up number is higher - I dont need a relationship in order to have sex with someone

Wow, no words

I don't think you really want to know and I don't think I want to tell you

C'mon I can take it, how many different people have you had sex with?

Men or women?

WTF seriously?

I been with girls, nothing ever romantically led to anything

Ok so how many women?

Like a half dozen

So you are bi?

No not at all

Well if you eat pussy I would have to categorize you as bi

Call me what you want

Well what is it?

It's not just about going down on girls, I'm not really even into that - it's the kissing, it's so sensual compared to men

And were these other women full blown lesbians, like butch dykes or were they just playin?

Some I think were all in

And are you over this phase in your life?

Yes if I find the right man I can't imagine doing it again, unless it's something he would want to introduce into our bedroom

So like did you go full double dong style?

What's that?

A double-ended dildo, you put it inside both of you then scissor

No, I never did that - some fingering w heavy make out sessions - just enough to get each other off - it's not like sex w men

And how many men have you had sex with?

I don't really want to say

It's that bad huh?

No I just don't think you can handle it

C'mon try me

I would rather lie to you to protect you

WTF it's that high of a number...like hundreds?

Maybe thousands...

Are you fucking kidding me right now?

Yes calm the fuck down

Sorry it's just that I am so jealous right now

Eighteen

18 men and 6 women?

6 women?

You said half a dozen

I guess

How can you know for certain 18 men but not sure about the number of women?

The women hook-ups involved booze, lots of it

So is that the key to get in your pants?

Please don't talk like that

Sorry I'm not saying you are a slut or anything

Well I have been slutty but that's not me now

Are you saying you had 18 separate boyfriends? That is a lot of relationships

No, like half were bfs, the others one night stands, or multiple night hook ups where there was chemistry but no emotional connection

I need a minute to wrap my feeble mind around this

Can I just say that my 'numbers' are fairly normal for any sensual American woman...look it up

It's not that, it's just our connection that was so tight in my mind now seems frayed by your past

My 'past' - that sounds rather condescending

I'm sorry

My past is who I am to this point now in my life. I have lived and lived without fear and repercussions. All of it, bad and good, made me who I am today. So if you like me now you like the things I went through to get here

Do you remember all of their names?

What kind of paranoid question is that?

I'm just curious

No I don't, it goes so far back. Don't worry, it's not like I am sitting around with these people in some spank bank recalling my time with them when I pleasure myself

Yeah that would be a concern?

A concern of what?

A concern going forward, like if we were to get together when this is over

You are unmasking yourself now, it's not a good look

What is a better look for you? Someone who doesn't give a shit about your body and your emotional baggage?

Emotional baggage from having a former sex life?

That and the comparing that you will now do

Oh now I get it, you are thinking like some porno script. So you are paranoid that I am comparing dicks when I have sex with someone?

I mean the more dudes you have been with the more dicks you have seen and this by calculation would mean you likely have seen some bigger than average

And you are paranoid that I am going to compare some donkey dick, that btw most women don't like, with your average cock?

In all honesty yes

What if I turn that around on you, how my pussy gonna feel versus the others you had? Can I get paranoid that mine might be bigger, looser, stinkier?

I doubt that

Or that my tits are small, or that I am better at eating pussy than sucking dick?

Whoa

It works both ways boo

Ok I think we should stop talking about this

I learned a lot about you today

Me? I am the one who now has your number in mind, forever burned into my frontal cortex

You asked, I told

I know, it's not your fault

Please don't call my past sex life my fault

I don't mean it that way

Ok nighty night

Talk tomorrow?

[conscious uncoupling refers to the act of ending a marriage or relationship, but in a way that is viewed as a very positive step by both parties, who believe that their lives will be better for doing so, and in order that they can continue to remain friends]

[gigolo: a derogatory term for a male escort or dancing partner, or a term used for a man who is supported by a woman in exchange for being her lover or escort]

[butch dykes can be used as an adjective or a noun to describe an individual's gender or gender preference. A masculine person of any gender can be described as butch, even though it is more common to use the term towards females with more masculine traits. The term butch tends to denote a degree of masculinity displayed by a female individual beyond what would be considered typical of a tomboy. It is not uncommon for women with a butch appearance to face harassment or violence. Surveys of butches showed that 50% were primarily attracted to femmes, while 25% reported being attracted to other butches. Butch dykes are the most recognizable public form of lesbianism while being the most outlaw figure within lesbian culture]

[The agreed upon ideal of lifetime sexual partners for an American woman is seven, while in all likelihood the actual number is likely a dozen]

[spank bank: a memorable collection of mental images that one retains for masturbatory purposes]

DAY●THIRTY FIVE

What happened to all of your hot virus talk?

I guess I'm over it

Did you have some brain injury I don't know about?

Am I not allowed to take a break from it?

I am happy for you, when this passes you will be able to transition back

Back to what?

To some normalcy, back to whatever it was you did before

That pre-virus life?

I've been thinking about those who have gone so hardcore, all in

The ones who drank the kool aid?

Yes, and those who are doubling down, even losing friends over it

Well I didn't have many friends before this

It has exposed a great divide in how we think

The left and right?

Yes, and then the more extreme

It all fell into political lines

And the script has flipped conventional logic of the parties

Oh?

Freedom loving liberals should be against all of the lockdowns and right wingers should be embracing the authoritarian essence

But it's the other way around

So much is being exposed, especially your media

My media?

Yes, yours and anyone who consumes it - not faulting you for that

They are not reporting on so much but you could argue that there is too much going on

I call BS on that one - they can prioritize, it's errors of omissions, purposefully leaving out what they don't want you to know - either for control or they think you can't handle the truth

Like the number of your sex partners?

Exactly, all those things that never get discussed for the safety of those involved LOL

Someone called CNN a tabloid

Sounds fitting

But so many hold it as the standard bearer

That is on them my friend

My friend, not my boo?

Sorry it's early, not fully there yet

Maybe the media landscape will be remade

I hope that some outlets are forced to shut down

Viewership is remarkably lower than most ppl think, primetime CNN shows are pulling numbers lower than random home repair shows

That's what I mean, I just want that closed down to allow for something new to replace it

What's up with you today?

Might just drink some wine and drunk text you later

Umkay, willing and waiting

● ● ●

What do you miss the most?

Everything

Obviously not sex cuz you got that

Ouch, are we going there?

No just kidding, still not over processing it, that's all

I miss going to work, and talking to coworkers

That's sad

Why?

Cuz it's like the one thing most ppl complain about

I know and I do, I don't actually like any of them but I feel a connection because I hear their stories about kids and pets and their dead bedrooms

Dead bedrooms?

The sexless marriages

Ppl talk about that? Do they talk about masturbation too?

No, why masturbation?

Idk it just seems like intimate talk for coworkers

I think you get comfortable in the mundane shell of a monotonous day to day grind, and within this you drone out, and your thoughts become part of the entire cog

Whoa

Did that make sense?

Yes, that's deep

So you relent with your own shields, letting them down, opening up, saying things that out of context would be shocking

Like what else?

Like this one girl I work w she is single and she disappeared one day for like half an hour, and comes back looking all disheveled and said she had just given a blowjob to the delivery driver in his truck, in the parking lot

Wow

And like this girl is not the type, she is even homely, heavier set, not full of self-confidence, but here she goes and does that and her first impulse is to come and brag about it to me

Could you get her fired for that?

Why would I want to do that?

Idk for being so slutty

If she wants to be slutty it's on her. She probably just needed the attention. Take it when you can

They say fat girls give the best head cuz they are making up for their bodies

That could be an exaggeration. Head game comes w experience

And the big girls like black guys

Or it's the black guys who like big girls

Why is that?

Maybe it has something to do w respect, or queen status, or big dicks making it through the fat thighs...or it's just what comes to be in the settlement of looks and the mating quotient

Mating quotient?

Like when someone is an 8 they usually go after other 8s

How about when an 8 is with a 2?

That's rare unless there is money involved

Or a big dick

Or mad blowjob skills

And this works when factoring in context, or race, even industry

Like?

Say a fat white girl decides to only date black men - she then goes from being a 4 to say an 8

But does the quality of men increase?

It might, but it's not about them, it's about her elevating her own status

And in industry?

So for example porn - yes, your favorite subject - some runaway chick makes it in the biz and she is the new "it" girl, ascending to 10 status, but in normal everyday life or back in high school they are like a 6 at best

Same goes for the dudes in porn too?

Yes even more so with them, with another multiplier of their dongs

LMFAO

Most are not even good looking on any level, like street 3s

Does personality matter?

Not really

What about with gays?

Yes so a hetero 4 woman goes lez and immediately becomes an 8 or 9

I have seen this, and honestly it pisses me off

What?

Like a really pretty girl that I am attracted to who is with a butch dyke type who is like a 2 on a good day

Happens all the time

It's not fair

Not saying it's fair, but maybe the pretty girl got tired of shit from men, or she is damaged goods, maybe she sees herself as a 2

I guess with all these ppl who level themselves upward there are those who go down

We don't all see ourselves the same way as others do

Any tips on how I can ascend the numbers?

Texting w a stranger is one way

I'm guessing you are a 9 and I am a 5

You can be whoever you want to be

Are we factoring in dongs?

If it helps in your numbers game, if not leave it out

Hypothetically and realistically I give myself 7 factoring in my personality

Can I answer the same, but factoring in my amazing pussy?

Sure...do elaborate

Nothing to see here but I've been told good things

Now you're getting me worked up and it's late and I am tired

Not trying to tease you boo

Too late for that

At least I got your mind off the virus

Yes thank god, I'm over it

And now you are visualizing what's behind the camel toe, those dampened folds of whiskery skin

Sounds inviting

The levels of viscosity

Sounds like an oil commercial

Depending where I am in my cycle

You mean blood?

No, like ovulation, when I get the wettest

Do tell

Almost too wet, like you wouldn't feel enough friction to cum

Test me

Or that perfect level after ovulation, two days before my first cramps

When you are just wet enough?

I'm always wet enough, just some moments I get too wet

Does this depend on who you are with?

Of course, can you get a boner for just anyone?

No there has to be some connection there, I am even mystified how porn actors can meet up on a set and minutes later be going at it

They will tell you it is all for show, that it's show business, that they are "working"

Still it's amazing

The girls are usually doped up, you can see it, and the guys are on viagra

Don't spoil it for me

Then the girl gets driven home by her suitcase bf, while the male actor returns to the gym and his roid regimen

Suitcase bf?

These are the loser boyfriends of the porn actresses, lowlifes who don't work, not even attractive guys, they drive the girls to set and wait for them outside, bringing them their phones between takes, power bars for lunch, scoring them coke

Wtf

Very common, maybe it reminds the girls of home, or being abused

Abused?

Yes these guys will beat the girls, they will live off of them and pay themselves for taking them to sets. For some of the girls they are so dead inside that being occasionally beaten, or abused on set, is the only thing they feel

Ewww

You didn't know this?

No, porn isn't like that for me

It's not about the porn, it's what you need to understand is involved in the process of making it

I'd rather not know, how do you even know this?

I like to read

Where do you read this?

It's out there, you just need to follow the threads

Some actresses seem to actually like the sex

I'm sure they do, I'm not trying to kill it for you, many of them it's just where they ended up...cute girls, molested by a relative, early exposure to drugs, ran away from home, went to LA, talentless but a nice pair of tits, did some stripping then got offered porn

You have to wonder what life post-porn is like

It's not good, back in the day actors could retire with their family never knowing about it, but now it's all over the internet and names can be searched, even aliases

It's more of that doubling down mentality, like w the virus lockdown pushers

Nice connection

Even though you know it's not sustainable or that it's not going to end well you turn off the future vision and double down on today

Reality deniers really

[to drink the kool-aid refers to followership at its worst. It was coined after a delusional, pseudo-guru named Jim Jones led his cult, the Peoples Temple, to mass suicide. Over 900 followers, including 304 children, killed themselves by drinking from a vat of a grape-flavored drink laced with cyanide]

[dead bedrooms are when couples evolve into a sexless relationship]

[mating quotient is the assigning of a numbered rating to potential sexual/romantic partners with a factored calculation of one's own level within the simplified 1 to 10 rankings]

[suitcase boyfriends, also known as suitcase pimps, are often real life boyfriends of porn actresses but could be a good friend or bodyguard, even an ex-lover. The relationship is an intimate one as he does her dirty work for her, including handling her money. Even though he may emotionally berate her or physically hurt her he cares about her and wants her to feel safe. The arrangement is typically unspoken and did not start out how it ended up being. It began with him dropping her off at shoots and picking her up later in the day, now he may be in charge of collecting her money and scoring her drugs. While becoming a permanent fixture in her life he becomes her de facto manager and in all certainty he is living off of her financially]

[dead inside is mostly used to describe when one feels numb, in a very negative way, but it can also be an emotional state that's based on defeat, feelings of helplessness, sadness or anger, and possibly shock]

DAY•THIRTY SIX

Good morning I lost you last night

My bad, I fell asleep while texting

I figured as much

So you were my last thought when I fell asleep

How endearing

I didn't want to bother you this morning in case you were sleeping off the wine

I was up early, meditation, yoga, shower, tea and some "me time"

Me time? You mean masturbation?

Um yeah but that's a big word

Self-love?

Just me time will suffice

Did you see that the projections may have been totally wrong?

What projections?

The original Ferguson/Imperial College numbers

What's that?

The original model that the govt used and relied on to shut it all down

The one that said millions would die?

Yes, over 2 million would die and the hospitals would be overrun

So that's now off?

Yes by orders of magnitude

What does that mean?

Like now the numbers of death will be the same as a bad flu season

How accurate is that?

Seems to be a fact, it's just not fully being presented in the media

Well ain't that some bullshit

We aren't going to hear about it, instead there will be a doubling down on the fear

At least, boo, this tells me that you have turned the corner in your processing of the spoonfed fear

Yes I'm seeing it clearer now

And that turns me on

Oh, it does?

It shows emotional intelligence

To be able to admit when you are wrong

I suppose there is that, but it's also that raw honesty that gets me moist

Ha, you said moist

Yeah what's up with the obsession with that word??

Some find it to be cringe-worthy, but I don't

I like it, it's a cool word

I like the imagery

What does it make you think?

In this context I think of your pussy

Ohhhh

But in general it might be the image of biting into a jelly-filled doughnut

What about the visual of me biting into a cream-filled maple bar and the cream oozes out onto my lips, and some of it drips into my cleavage

There is that

But I digress, it's too early to talk like that

Now that you got me worked up?

Just shutting it down before it becomes too much

Throttling the discourse, like you do so well

I'm just containing myself, I don't want to rub one out so soon after the last session. I am conscious of my sensitivity levels

Girls do that too?

Do what?

Space out their beat off sessions?

I guess, we leave it to desire and if it's there. We never really force it

Admittedly I find myself forcing it often. I think it's cuz we are so visual. I might have some thought of a naked woman, imagining some chick I see on the street or an aspect of some 'performer' I like and then it causes the reels to play out

You can still get hard?

It gets difficult if it's like the third or fourth time that day

Wow that's concerning

Ok that would be an extreme day, of lockdown mind you

So what's your regular beat off sched?

I guess once a day but if I'm dating someone maybe zero, so I have the stamina to perform IRL

IRL?

In real life

Is that gamer code talk?

I don't think so, but it's definitely a term for the virtuals among us

When you say 'dating' someone do you mean like a real relationship or something more casual sex like

Are you jealous now?

No I want to understand what you mean

Well, you need names and numbers?

No, what does it mean 'dating'?

Like the last girl I was with she never met my mother. I met her online, we met up for coffee, she came over for the next date and we made out on the couch then had sex. We didn't see eye to eye on much but the sex was satisfactory enough that we did it a few more times. During that time frame we were dating. I have the dates in my calendar if you are interested

Um no thanks

You jealous now?

No, just way more questions but I got to go, someone is calling

• • •

How many other girls have you dated?

You want my number now?

No just curious, not jealous at all

Well it's more than one and less than your total, and my total is only chicks no dudes

I didn't think there would be dudes

And no chicks with dicks either

Whoa I didn't think that either

Well in case you thought I liked that sort of thing

Why would I think that?

Idk it's popular stuff

What's that, women who have dicks?

Well they are really dudes with tits, but yes

Whatever floats your boat

It doesn't float mine

What do you like?

I think I like authentically feminine girls, meaning girly, with high pitched voices, busty, bigger asses

Do you like the naughty librarian look or something more home girl style?

Is this a porno set up?

No just your overall ideal look

I'm easy, I think it comes down to personality

And big titties of course

You jealous now? I am guessing yours aren't that big

Please never talk to a lady like that

Sorry, I mean I am putting the clues together

Mine certainly are not big by any means but they exist and they are supple and my nipples are exquisite, so there is that

Sounds legit

My tits are legit now?

Well it always seems like w women there are pluses and minuses, like small tits nice nipples, or no tits but exquisite ass, or overall great body but fugly face, those we call butterfaces, everything but her face...or beautiful face w blahh body

Ouch, could I possibly have it all in one package?

Send pics and I will comment

[order of magnitude is the scale of everything, beginning with spacetime, or quantum foam, and moves through small elementary particles, intermediate elementary particles, large elementary particles, components of composite particles, the components of atoms, electromagnetic waves, simple atoms, complex atoms, molecules, small viruses, large viruses, chromosomes, cells, hairs, body parts, species, groups of species, small areas such as craters, large areas such as land masses, planets, orbits, stars, small planetary systems, intermediate planetary systems, large planetary systems, collections of stars, star clusters, galaxies, galaxy groups, galaxy clusters, galaxy superclusters, the cosmic web, Hubble volumes, and ends with the Universe]

[emotional intelligence is the capability of individuals to recognize their own emotions and those of others, discern between different feelings and label them appropriately while using emotional information to guide thinking and behavior, managing and/or adjusting emotions to adapt to environments in order to achieve one's goal]

[moist is an adjective, moist·er, moist·est; meaning moderately or slightly wet; damp. It can be used to say you are ill informed or have said something idiotic or embarrassing. Moist can also be used to describe a situation or occurrence. If someone is faced with a circumstance that is particularly displeasing it's also acceptable to say something like 'gurl that's moist']

[Butter face: A homonym that sounds like "but her face." To call a woman a "butter face" is to say her body is very sexy but her face is ugly]

DAY•THIRTY SEVEN

They are starting to call this Generation Pandemic

Who are they?

Mostly the magazines this week

It's catchy

All part of the narrative

Of course, and the encompassing safe space inclusionary concept

What?

It makes you feel like you are part of something. Tribalism

Even if it's something lame?

Yes, it's not lame for them, it's a badge of honor

Like they don't know better?

That and they don't know anything else - so you get enveloped into the movement

It's an easy sell when it's the only thing for sale

Then the push for solidarity becomes easy, and a call to action with a collective disgust for anything that runs contrary

Like some psy-ops experiment

Exactly, but it's a real life event unfolding before us, no experiment needed

Then the resulting division from the deepening of party lines and more hardcore stances

It's all about division, that's what politicians do best - keep the ppl fighting so they don't question anything else

Like setting the dumpster on fire and standing back in the crowd watching it burn

The pyro in the audience - there is some of that

Can we ever get back to how it was?

How was it?

Ppl nicer to each other, civility

I don't think so but why would we even want to at this point?

It's a point of no return?

Yes, too much has been exposed, and there is more to come

Like what?

The media have been exposed as nothing more than fear mongers for ratings, politicians have been exposed as knowing nothing more than you and me, and the biggest is the gullibility factor of ppl on highlighted display

People are dumb, there I said it

Yeah most are, but it's easy for us to sit here and wax poetic on the randoms and their levels of intelligence without sounding douchey ourselves

It's not just that they are dumb, they lack knowledge and most importantly instinct, or if they do have instinct it's either wrong or they are not following up on it

So here we have Generation Pandemic that we could also call Generation Sheeple but that's condescending and rude

After the hysteria can we have some distance to assess the damage?

● ● ●

Want to hear about this kinda intimate thing I do?

Has someone been drinking?

Maybe a little bit

Yes, do tell, I'm just sitting here on the couch watching the sunset through the window

It usually requires a bottle of wine in my system, but what I do is I get a full length mirror

And?

And I may start with a sort of strip tease in the mirror, a show for myself, sounds weird, but I just make moves that I feel in the moment, no music, almost like a silent disco

Video or it didn't happen

Then I strip all the way down to full nude

Ok

Then I begin a self-examination of my nude body, I know this sounds weird

No not at all

I start with my face, pulling back my hair tight and hard, giving my face a good stretch, like a facelift, pulling the wrinkles on my forehead

I'm sure it's not that bad

Then I pull back on my ears to tighten my cheeks and this pulls my mouth into a pouty smirk, almost like a sex doll, w her mouth ready to suck

I like it

Then I run my fingers along the length of my collarbone and arms looking for moles or anything on my skin that is new

Ok please tell me you don't find anything

Then to the breast exam, where I administer my own mammogram, rolling the fat of my tits in my hands like a ball of dough, I don't do it hard enough to hurt, and what's left is my nipples becoming erect

Ski slopes?

What's that?

Like in their silhouette your breasts suspend like a ski slope, with the arch of your nipple the jumping off point

Yeah kinda. Then I run my fingers down the length of my tummy, and dip a fingertip into my belly button to check for lint. I feel for the abs that are hard underneath the thin layer of flab. I consciously acknowledge that I need to be more intense in my workouts

I'm sure it's not that bad

Then I slide my hands down the side of my outer thighs, like a gunslinger reaching for his pistols, then around the front side to grab onto the chub of my inner thighs, that place where the thigh gap goes

I'm sure it's not that bad

Then I grab it hard, like a big pinch, like I'm angry at it, like I am pissed and want it gone. I paint a picture in my mind of it poppin like a water balloon

Ouch

Then I bend slightly forward and run my soft hands over the rough skin of my knee caps then fully down to my ankles which I grab onto, stretching out my glutes, feeling the freon of the AC blowing onto my vagina

Umkay

Then I stand back up again and move closer to the mirror and this is when I go full gyno exam, parting my labia majora and looking at the pink circle of my vagina's entrance

I'm sure it's tight, looks like a pink balloon knot

Um no, it looks like a pink volcano ready to erupt. Then I process all that has been inside of me, all the abuse my pussy has taken, both for good and bad. Those times I didn't want to do it, those times when it hurt, all the tampons that have been inside me, the carrots, the cucumbers, dildoes and vibrators, tongues, dicks and fingers. The toxic shock and urinary tract infections

But doesnt it work like a self-cleaning oven?

It does do wonders and will take care of itself, but you can't introduce ingredients into the dish...salt water sex will throw off the pH balance, or douches are the worse

How do you keep the smell down?

What smell?

You know if it gets funky

That doesn't happen cuz I soap it and wipe well and eat a clean diet

The funky ones are probably the neglected ones

Um mine is pretty neglected LOL but I know what you mean

Tease

I might come across a stray hair that's like an inch long where the rest of my pubes are either shaved smooth or a small stubble, like 3-day growth at worse

Is there a landing strip?

No and the 90s called and they want their pubescape back lmfao

So that's not a thing now?

All my girlfriends are fully bare, it feels better, cleaner, and it's what the guys like - I'm sure pubes will make a comeback - maybe pandemic pubes LOL where some girls just let it all grow out in isolation

Yeah guys like to keep their own pubes trimmed to make their dicks look bigger, or so I heard

And girls don't like to choke out on pubes

There is that

And then for my final mirror act I turn around and stick my ass out to the mirror, reaching back and parting my ass cheeks, and take in the view of my asshole, taint and pussy. What it looks like from back there. I think of all that comes out of me comes through here. All the shit and waste my body sends away. I wonder if the small hole of my ass looks cute to guys who do me doggy style. I am amazed at how such big shits can come from such a hole. And wonder if my pussy lips are not too big for my age...

No self love at this point?

No, then I wrap it up by getting dressed and processing a general sense of gratitude for what I am working with, even if it seems inferior to others

I'm sure it's not

Like when I think that my left tit is a full cup smaller than my right, I think of those who have had breast cancer and had mastectomies

Ouch

Or when I think of being fat I recognize that I can still feel the firmness of the abs behind the flab, so I am close

Have you seen an American woman lately?

Or how my hips flare outward when I bend forward and the overall aesthetic brings a narrowness to my lower backside, that it's the most flattering sign of femininity, and that men love it, and I have it

All this hot talk has got me bothered

Sorry for teasing you, why don't you just rub one out?

I might have to later, but not while I'm typing back to you

I will let you go now, I'm buzzed and ready to pass out

Night boo, talk tomorrow

[Generation Pandemic's story has yet to be told. We know the crisis will have a lasting effect; we just don't know how severe it will be. A prolonged experience, highly contagious and unpredictable, the virus has upended their education, social relationships, and family lives. Depending on resiliency this may result in some kids being able to pull themselves out of multigenerational cycles of poverty, or it could go the other direction with a deepening of the chasmic gap between the affluent children and those that come from poverty, ultimately affecting a remapping of the near future]

[tribalism is the state of being organized by, or advocating for, tribes or tribal lifestyles. Human evolution has primarily occurred in small groups, as opposed to mass societies, and humans naturally maintain a small social network]

[Pyromania is an impulse control disorder in which individuals repeatedly fail to resist impulses to deliberately start fires, in order to relieve tension or for instant gratification. The term pyromania comes from the Greek word πῦρ (pyr, fire). Pyromania is distinct from arson, the deliberate setting of fires for personal, monetary or political gain. Pyromaniacs start fires to induce euphoria, and often fixate on institutions of fire control like fire stations and firemen, often staying at the scene of the crime to watch the firemen put the fire out]

[gullibility is a failure of social intelligence in which a person is easily tricked or manipulated into an ill-advised course of action. It is closely related to credulity, which is the tendency to believe unlikely propositions that are unsupported by evidence]

[sheeple: noun (plural only); derogatory, slang; people who unquestioningly accept as true whatever their political leaders say or who adopt popular opinion as their own without scrutiny]

[thigh gap is a gap between the thighs, caused either naturally or through exercise and healthy eating habits; a much sought after body characteristic, it was popularized in the late Aughts when Western female magazines began to focus on the thigh gap as a feature of peak physical attractiveness]

[landing strip pubescapes originated in the 1980s as a counter to the full bush aesthetic of the prior decade. For females now the appeal is that they can go almost totally bare yet say "Hey there, I am capable of growing pubic hair, I just don't have it right now." It's for when you want to be completely hairless yet still look or feel like a grown woman. There are two popular styles, floating, where it it sits above the vagina like an island, or anchored deeper into the labia folds]

DAY●THIRTY EIGHT

That was a loaded evening, sorry about that

No apologies needed

I kinda revealed too much, looking back at the texts I come off as a crazed egomaniac

Not at all, maybe just a big tease

You liked that?

Oh yes I did

Men are sick lol

We are visual creatures and we like the female body, at least most of us do, so

I guess for women it's more about a feeling, and other senses involved, like scent or pressure, even pain can get us off

Here we go again

No it's way too early for hot talk, and I'm hungover, what I mean is for us it's an all encompassing process

I get it, we can beat off to a picture of a woman in a bikini, or to scrambled muted porn

Muted porn?

Yeah porn without sound

Oh, I like to hear the actors though, and the ridiculous noises they make. I could actually get myself off just listening without visuals

It gets annoying to me, how many times can you scream oh god, or moan ah ah ah

It's all part of the presentation - don't you make some noise when you fuck?

I guess not, now that I think about it

I'm not loud but I'm not quiet either, I don't hold back, if I'm enjoying it I will let you know

Here we go

No I'm not going there this early and today is not going to be a day drinking day

What are your plans?

I'm gonna venture out for groceries

Ooh exciting

And see what's the scene on the streets and report back to you

Be sure to take a mask, I heard businesses are requiring them in order to enter

I don't have one

Just wrap a thong around your face

Would that work?

Probably nobody would say anything, I certainly wouldn't

Sounds kinda like performance art

Or just tell them to fuck off

Ouch I would never

I don't think anyone is allowed to make someone else wear a mask

Maybe so but for civility I will do it, or just not go where I need one

I'm seeing lots of talk about how this virus will penetrate right through a mask, like putting a chain link fence up to protect against mosquitoes

Lmfao

But hey if it gives someone a sense of safety, or the idea that they are not infringing on others with their toxic breath then go on w your bad selves

I see an interesting turn of thoughts from you

Oh I haven't really changed

Yes you have, you are more direct and less clouded by what you see around you, maybe the media manipulation isn't working so well on you anymore

I think it is a clarity that comes w five weeks of isolation

It's been strange indeed, has it been that long?

Yes, with no end in sight

It will end eventually, just like everything

And then the new normal

Maybe a new new normal that is somewhat close to what we had before

We can only dream

[Various types of face masks available to the general public are worn for protection against inhalation of dust, pollutants, allergens, and organisms. These masks will not protect against highly pathogenic influenza or other virus outbreaks as illustrated by the ineffective widespread use of face masks for protection against the global virus outbreaks over the last few decades]

[new normal is originally a business and economics term but applicable to the change that comes about after extraordinary events, giving way to a newfound vigilance against future contagions, signaling the end of hugging or handshakes]

DAY●THIRTY NINE

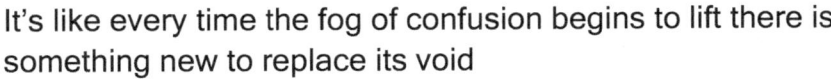

It's like every time the fog of confusion begins to lift there is something new to replace its void

Good morning to you

How did you sleep?

Well, as per the usual, and you?

Fine I just woke up in a foul mood

I think it's normal, we are all in this together

So much doesn't make sense to me and it's not like we are getting any answers

From who, the govt? Lmfao

From anyone, it's like a moveable feast of triggers

If ppl are looking to be offended or scared they will find it, believe me, they don't need guidance

Yeah, so it doesn't matter if you are trying to appease anyone, there will always be the outliers

There are ppl like a whack a mole just waiting for the signal

That's why most of this doesn't matter, it's like thousands could die and they would be happy, nobody dies and they are angry that the predictions didn't come through

Like damned if you do and damned if you don't and damned if you tried

Yes, I have had friends like that and I finally had to cut ties

We can't just placate every motherfucker, even if we could

Ha, true dat

Their own issues are theirs to resolve

But the problem is they won't resolve them, they will just double down, and be further emboldened by those within their tribe

And so-called adults are allowed to infiltrate public policy and dictate how everyone should feel

Pretty much, and take their leads from politicians that are using them as pawns within their political theater

They are getting played and not even knowing it

Exactly, fully played, having their emotions manipulated by the fear onslaught, by the media looking for numbers. It's because their minds are weak, because they are scared to think for themselves, and just want to be told how to think

Wow, slay it gurl

Blistering commentary right there but obviously true when you cut through all the bullshit, it really is all that is left

And they are becoming more unmasked each day

But it won't matter because they will cover themselves up with something new, a projection onto thee, or that they are no longer afraid for themselves just for the elderly and the sick. That you are being insensitive because you are anything less than totally afraid. The 'how dare you' mindset type of shit - shaming as well

So they cover it up, like with their tattoos and piercings, another form of masking

There could be that, you can learn a lot from looking at a person

And you can learn what not to do lol

Yes, on the surface the clues are all there

Like what?

Traces and remaining evidence of sexual abuse, much of it in the obesity

So fat ppl are sex abuse survivors?

Not all, but much of them are. When you get traumatized like that as a kid you try and put on some weight to keep the predators at bay

Like contact tracers?

Ouch, I see what you did there - yeah anything to stop the contact - so a little girl might pack on the weight, parents explain it off as a thyroid issue and she ends up in adulthood w type 2 diabetes

The infamous co-morbidities

Same applies to boys - studies have shown that the stress of childhood trauma events will destroy aspects of the immune system, so that the obesity goes further unfettered

Like unchained body mass?

Yes so the typical regulators we all have will stop a person from getting too big because there is something about a drip system into the metabolism process, that can be choked off by the actual trauma - so it ends up being a double edged sword

Yeah sometimes I see ppl and I am like wtf happened here, sorry but true

I get it, I too wonder how some get to this point, and this is often the path to it...and for tattoos there is the idea that you are inking yourself to take back ownership of your body

Um, do you have any tats?

Maybe, and you?

Zero, ink free - I mean I'm open to it if you were into it on men?

So you would tat yourself just for me? How sweet

What is yours?

Just something small that I regret, maybe I will show you sometime

Now we are talking - I need a brighter visual for the day

Not interested in the hot obesity abuse talk?

I like your theories it's just that I don't want that shit clouding my mind for the day

This is why I always have sympathy for the extremely obese, it's like I know something happened to them, and they are wearing it for us to figure out, or at least as a signal to not do more harm

Sometimes I see certain ppl and think if I was that big, that 1, I would never leave the house, 2 I would try and do something about it

But see, often they cannot. It's not even about what they eat. The food is not processing properly

And they say exercise is more about health and not a real way to lose weight

Some may not want to lose it, there are the feeder types, where a woman may be fetishized by her weight, and there are men paying her to eat in front of them

Wtf?

Look it up on your porn channels

Sex with food?

No, sexual thrill from watching a 400 pound woman in a negligee eat an entire cake

Wow, there really are no bounds

And there are those who, again, are just doubling down because it is the easier path, at least it is easier in their minds. Go deeper with the weight, as opposed to the immense struggle required to lose it. This applies to science deniers, and to gender activists, or 'believe all accuser' types. It's about doubling down until the attention is off the topic. Almost like a religion

I see what you are saying, and on a similar thread I could see that happening w the virus where there is a pandemonium

fever pitch then abracadabra, the summer heat makes it disappear

Onto the next cause of concern

There are already rumblings of an entirely new virus, NOT a second wave, but a completely unrelated new strain coming this fall

How could they know about such a thing?

Good question, and good questions never get asked

It's all about innuendo and feelings

Doesn't it seem like a massive psychological operation on the American mind?

Yes, but that's been going on for years, now it's just reached fever pitch levels

Peak gaslighting from all sides

Yes, and w gaslighting the best response is no response, what the victims of narcissists call 'grey rocking'

Whoah, lol

Look at the news, then look at the online virtue signalers that take what they are fed then repackage it...look at them as nothing more than narcissists baiting for a reaction

Even the fugly online influencers?

Especially those, narcissism does not mean you are attractive, and that is the biggest danger cuz you least expect it

So it's not just the hot chicks?

Often it's not hot chicks at all, those are the ones w the most insecurities, they are the ugly ducklings that turned for the attractive, those are the women who now never get asked out

Who would want to deal with their drama?

Usually they are drama free fyi - do you have no faith in me?

So you are saying someone who has let themselves go to hell physically is potentially a narcissist?

Yes, they will take every opportunity to dogmatically impose their way of thinking onto you, covertly or overtly

Then they must be everywhere

Yes they are. So back to them and their virtue signaling, the best is to not bite, don't take the bait, don't react, don't make any rash decisions based off of their posture or stance

This is grey rocking?

Yes it's like you are acting how a rock would react

Dead inside?

If you want, but basically it is ZERO reaction

But then they might get pissed at you

No, surprisingly they don't even notice, mostly because it's all about them, and how they feel, and if you are putting them in danger, or if you think differently politically....so the approach is best to roll with it...why do you need to win? Why would you need to bother trying to talk them down off a ledge of their own idiocy?

Good point, sounds like you studied psycho therapy

No but I did date a psycho and it went bad

Do tell

How much time have you got?

All day boo

Let me get some wine going lol

Anything you need

So he was damaged goods, I just didn't see it at the time...average looking, you need to know that looks are not that important to me

I hope not

And now in retrospect it's like one of those flashback scenes from a movie where I see all the red flags and because I was naive to the manipulation I was pulled deeper into his web of deceit and what I learned later was his shattered ego

Then what?

It started with him isolating me from friends and family. He would make snide judgmental remarks about them, and I would believe what he was saying

Like what?

Like how a certain girlfriend was dangerous because she was so jealous she was basically out to get me. Or how my own family didn't give a shit about me. So some of it made sense, like if you use general platitudes it will hit on a nerve, like fortune tellers who cast a wide net with their proclamations

But did you act on it?

In my mind I did, I became paranoid about those around me

Why was he doing this to you?

I guess because of his own insecurities. It's what narcissists do, they don't want those around them to flourish in any way

I am seeing so much of this online, in the socials

Yes, in times like this it becomes apparent, that is if you know what to look for

Most of it is stuff that doesn't make sense to me, like a young healthy person who is trying to strike fear in other young healthy people, when the numbers just aren't there

Yeah it's like a 'how dare you live' phenomenon, classic narcissism

Then what happened to this guy?

He started showing his own insecurities, and luckily I was conscious of it and able to fully comprehend what he was up to, so I became cold toward him

Like no more sex?

The sex was never good or frequent to begin with. Sex is actually a litmus test for one's own self esteem or lack thereof. It's just you there w the other person, nobody to blame, no hype squad, just the ability to make someone feel a certain way or not

Like you can't fake sexual skills?

No you cannot, and he wasn't good at it. I mean I can't really remember it at all, and that should tell you something. So I slowly blew him off, acting dead inside around him...I went from this bubbly persona to quiet and introverted over a matter of days and he never even noticed

What did you do?

I just stopped talking about myself. That is part of the grey rock, is you no longer give up info about yourself, you essentially take away anything they can use as ammo at a later date

Let me guess, he still didn't notice?

No, instead it seemed to empower him by giving him more oxygen to air his own magnificence

What a douche!

Yes he was a douche on many levels, then when they realize YOU are not doing it for THEM any longer they lose interest in you and move on. In break ups like this they tend to turn it back around on themselves, saying it's not you, it's them blah blah

And on to the next victim?

Yes, but this doesn't work in families where ppl are stuck, and this is when parents can keep their children down, or on the wrong path

Now you got me thinking

Isn't it interesting how it triggers a flashback to your life and those pivotal moments?

Yeah it's deep, I don't know if I want to go there

It's the best thing you could do for yourself boo

I might need to visit a therapist when the lockdown lifts

You don't need a therapist when you got me

I don't know how deep you would want to go, or how exposed I would want to feel around you

Try me

[outlier: in statistics, it is a data point that differs significantly from other observations. An outlier may be due to variability in the measurement or it may indicate experimental error; the latter are sometimes excluded from the data set. An outlier can cause serious problems in statistical analyses. The word can be used with more metaphorical flexibility, describing a truly exceptional individual who, in his or her field of expertise, is so superior that he defines his own category of success]

[true dat: African American vernacular for "that is true"]

[political theater: overblown reactions, campaign promises that can't be kept, and sensationalized news stories spun in bias so as to create a false narrative during an election cycle;

propaganda a political candidate uses to their advantage; a
fake attitude to gain supporters such as pandering]

[feederism is an underground sexual fetish which involves
one partner (the feeder) feeding the other, both to obtain
sexual arousal and to encourage weight gain in the feedee.
Feederism can vary in nature, from a consensual act between
two people who mutually appreciate a larger body type, to
non-consensual abuse, which may involve force-feeding and
bondage and is undertaken with the intention of fattening up
the feedee to the point of immobility and total dependence.
The weight gained can also vary from a few pounds to
hundreds, whilst some feeder relationships are not undertaken
with the purpose of weight gain at all but for the enjoyment of
food in an intimate context. Most feedees are female (BBW or
SSBBW) whilst the feeders tend to be males; gay/lesbian
feeder relationships are not entirely uncommon]

[fever pitch: a state of extreme excitement]

[gaslighting: a form of psychological manipulation in which a
person or a group covertly sows seeds of doubt in a targeted
individual or group, making them question their own memory,
perception, or judgment, often evoking in them cognitive
dissonance and other changes including low self-esteem]

[grey rocking: is a technique for interacting with manipulative
and abusive people, including those with narcissistic
personality disorder or antisocial personality disorder as well

as toxic people without a mental health diagnosis. The strategy involves becoming the most boring and uninteresting person you can be when interacting with a manipulative person since people with manipulative personalities feed on drama, the duller and more boring you seem the more you undermine their efforts to control you]

DAYFORTY

You up yet?

Um yes, why wouldn't I be?

Well I thought you'd text me by now

It's my job to start?

Not really but I never wanted to bother you so early so I always let you send the first one

That's sweet but it's like you are leaving me out to dry

How is that?

What if i am sitting here wondering if you even want to talk, and I have to be the first one to start it

Never hesitate on hitting me up, seriously

When life returns to the new normal we won't have this time to message each other

In that case I don't want the lockdown to end

It certainly is nice to wake up and have zero plans

I miss the grind of having tasks, but that's probably just a guy thing

Consider me one of your tasks

Oh yeah

Like to entertain me is task number one for the day

So am I doing a good job ma'am?

I would say so, if you need punishment I will let you know

Um now I'm listening

You weren't listening before?

I was but now I'm going into reading between the lines, looking at your emotions through the text, and analyzing what you may intentionally be leaving out of the message

Ok sigmund freud

Sometimes it's about what people don't say that matters most

Yeah but maybe they are not saying it because there is nothing there

Sure but it's fun to fill in the blanks

So when I am adamant and say 'no nudes' what do you take away?

I immediately add the word 'yet' to the message. There is always the possibility for a change in mindset

That's confident of you

Sure but I have lived enough in life to believe in laws of attraction and the power to manifest what you desire

You turning new age on me?

No but I am comfortable enough to share with you this way of my thinking

I like it, it turns me on

This is where I fill in my mind the thought of your lady parts getting moist

Ok that use of words all together is odd and off putting

I didn't want to be crass

Just say I imagine your pussy is getting wet

Yes that is better just didn't want to offend

I know it's early but c'mon you know I'm cool with it

So when I imagine in my mind a fully played out scene this leads to me being more at ease, as well as putting out a gravitational pull for the event to come to me

This does not sound at all like incel talk

Do you still think I'm an incel?

Kinda, to be honest

Well time to move on from that

I will at some point, but I'm still vetting you

I don't know too many incels but they dont speak like me, they have a very low level of emotional intelligence

I would give you a 6 or 7 in that dept, but it would depend on the factor of your age

Do you really want to know?

No, not yet. Keep it from me, seriously

I wasn't planning on it. And I don't want to know yours. I have a pretty good idea though

Oh yes?

I think you are older than me

Well duh

It's just a question of how much

● ● ●

Did you see the story about the new kid virus?

Yes and I immediately dismissed it

Why?

Because it came out on the heels of certain govt heads talking about not reopening schools this year

So it's more of a scare tactic?

Timing wise yes

If the schools stay closed then parents have to stay home and the economy suffers more

Well I was gonna tell you, this disease, kawasaki syndrome, they were saying it's related to the virus, and they even had all these stories lined up about how it hit preschools around the world, but then it got debunked as an extremely rare disorder, like something that only affects a dozen kids EVERY decade or so

It's good to see the stories being debunked before they can get too widespread

Almost like whack a mole or putting out a fire

At this point I dont even blame the media, they dont hide their agenda nor the fact that they are private businesses looking for viewers....I blame the public for being so dumb

Preach it

The level of gullibility is just too much, it makes me glad I am so isolated because I just can't imagine in-person conversations with anyone who is buying the narrative

What about all the elderlies dying?

There is that and I don't deny it but throw in age and our fav word "co-morbidities"

Im just playin, I'm with you...I don't know how anyone CANNOT question the narrative

Maybe there is comfort in it

Or it's a missing part of the brain, that part that questions existence

That could be it, or too much reptilian brain parts letting them be scared into a private oblivion

Or a general willingness to conform, what's up with that? It's kinda opposite of American thinking

Oh but that could be considered patriotic and therefore triggering LOL

Acquiescing to The Man was always something that could garner revolt, now it's all about the serfdom placating the rulers

Nobody questions the rulers either, these are regular people who have been handed immense power because of the situation

Maybe the situation was "manufactured" so the power could be tapped into?

That works as a concept IF there is something more to this, another strain of cause and effect taking place that we don't know about

There is so much we don't know about

Like what could these forces do or implement with the vast majority of the people under house arrest

Maybe indictments on high levels and quick arrests

What about the destruction of brick and mortar society

Or mandated vaccines that will kill off 20 percent of the population

The Club of Rome?

What's that?

A group that has been advocating for hundreds of years to lower the world population, that the planet would be much better off if it had half the people

Is it based in Rome?

Originally yes, it was a group of ex popes and renaissance families, now it's made up of global elites

I don't see how they could kill 3 or 4 billion ppl

They can't really, they have tried though

Oh, how?

The Black Plague was *supposedly* set off by them, but then there was the triggering of WW1 and that was supposed to do it. Then that war didn't do it so it was all about a nuclear war, and a subsequent nuclear winter taking out half the population

But kinda doesn't make sense because the ppl instigating it could get killed too

They would be hidden away for the duration, or protected by a top secret inoculation

Sounds pretty far fetched

It does but the group is real and there is no doubting that

Let me guess, now they operate under an environmentalist cover?

Yes, and it allows them to recruit the young

Do you think this virus is their work?

No but I could see the vaccine that could get mandated as their work. It could have a backdoor aspect that could kill off certain populations

Oh?

Like third and fourth world peeps

Peeps?

If the lockdown goes much longer I will volunteer for the trials

Like a vaccine that could kill you?

I don't think it would do that on me, in my health

What's to say the 3rd worlder doesn't have a stronger system than you?

They might, like the homeless, they haven't gotten hit hard by the virus because they have such strong immune systems

Ewww

Ewww what?

I just imagine them eating out of trash cans and wearing soiled clothes

Yes that's what they do

For some reason I just want to barf a little in my mouth when I think of them

No sympathy?

Yes of course, but I can't help myself - even when I pass them by on a sidewalk I have to hold my breath

It's amazing how much the human body can endure, the abuse it can take

Yeah, I'm sure some of these ppl could be cleaned up and apart from sunburns or advanced aging look somewhat normal

Like the mating quotient, there is the street version, when you say they are a 'hard 30' and look fifty

They are the living manifestation of bad choices and the results

But some are victims

Yes and then instead of rising up from that fate they allowed themselves to be taken by it

Surely there are horror stories that you could never imagine

I'm just saying there was a point, a bad decision, where they rolled with the punches

Victim versus victor

Exactly, but even that could be clouded by trauma or drug use, anything to escape from brutal reality

Some of it is even just being dumb, not like in a bad way, just ignorance

When you are raised without any skill set for dealing and coping with life

Without the process for making beneficial choices, when life as a shit show is somehow embraced

Like white trash chic or praise for losers?

Exactly, there is that low grade verve in American culture that somehow glorifies being dumb

It works if you are rich or somehow buffered with safety nets but it can go off the rails rather quickly when you become exposed

Being exposed really is what's going on now all around us

It is all out there if you are looking

The inability of politicians, the lack of celebrity, no sports, no big movies, and nobody seems bothered

The big reveal

Of what?

Of it all, like an emperor has no clothes moment

The "scientists" keep getting their projections wrong and then they blame bad data, the same data that we are supposed to live and die by, as if it's somehow a circular firing squad of blame, and if you are so inclined you must take a side

That's the thing, you don't have to take a side

Not in our binary world

You can still think freely, have your own political beliefs that don't fall into a right or left leaning line

You wouldn't think that was possible if you are online...have you been online lately?

Yes it's a shitshow of mudslinging and allegations mostly rooted in emotions and disinformation

Bwahaha so true, the factor of some dumb fuck all juiced up on dopamine mainlining from his false sense of audience going full virtue signal for more justification of his own madness

Or something like that

Yes it comes in many forms but it's the same type of person

I find them to be too much

Like you can't handle it?

I can't handle it and I feel sorry for them and those around them. They are petulant brats

Lmfao

Really that is all it is, some ignoramus who has a very small microphone through social media bloviating their disgust on some topic then the slow drip of praise back at them within their own echo chamber

Ha so true

It's almost like an experiment in masturbation

Do tell

That's it, it's masturbatory behavior

I thought you were taking this convo to another level

I haven't had my wine

Well get on it

I will text you later, charge your phone

• • •

Um did you see that the govt releases footage of UFOs, and actually declared officially that these are indeed Unidentified Flying Objects and absolute crickets from the media

I saw that but I was confused, I thought it was something old that had already been released

Ok if so, how would that have changed the response?

Idk like it gets diluted with all that's going on

Ok official unidentified flying objects is an 11 while this virus BS is a 3

Good point, it seems once the story is like a day old it loses its luster

We are losing our perspective in this country, and history is dead

I'm listening

Listening to what?

Your story about the UFOs

Well it's Navy footage that shows these objects flying at speeds unknown to man, zipping through the sky, darting around kinda like a surveillance mission

Any ideas that it could be fake?

Zero, and why would the govt declassify something fake like that? It's not like it's working as a distraction, nobody is batting an eye

So here is the thing with aliens...if we are to confirm their existence it completely decimates the essence of religion

Yes, not just that but then we collectively need to be really concerned

And it has been revealed w this virus that globally it's like every country is on its own

So what happens if we were to come under attack?

I think we would take the lead, we have a Space Force after all LOL

And then protect just North America?

We wouldn't protect shit because whatever weapons they have would render us completely impotent

Impotent lol

So there would be no battles, just surrender

Maybe they wouldnt be interested in us, like we may be too dumb, too primitive

It probably would come down to minerals, if earth has something they need, or fuel

I always had this idea that for two separate planets to simultaneously exist with some form of advanced life would be such a rare event in the totality of space time

Like we take turns existing?

Kinda but then with all the talk of these goldilocks systems of planets, that there are millions of planets that could sustain life I thought there must actually be many planets, but that the current situation of the form of life is varied, like some are simply microbes, while some may be post-humanoid

Post-humanoid?

Like the typical aliens we see, maybe a life form that is 20 million years past our own evolution

Interesting, big picture approach

You have to go big picture when you talk of the universe, anything on our limited cognitive level cannot make logic of it

We are a mere blip on the screen

If you laid out the existence of earth, the 4 or 5 billion years onto a calendar starting January 1 through December 31, the existence of HUMANS takes place only in the final 1 minute of New Year's Eve

Wow

And if you believe in any of the STAR PEOPLE talk then life elsewhere makes sense

Star people?

The idea that we are actually Martians

Wtf

That star seeds hit earth, through some form of Mars colliding with earth at some point, or our moon bouncing off of earth with the seedlings of life from a prior collision with Mars

That's out there thinking

Yes it is and it's big in the New Age circles so nobody takes it seriously, buuuut it kinda makes sense

Simply put, something needed to seed earth

Exactly, so why not from elsewhere, and if that is the case then that source life is evolving as well, but perhaps on a way more advanced time space continuum

So these aliens have evolved with their big heads and 3 fingers?

Could be, bigger heads for bigger brains, lose some digits cuz we dont need all 5

Speak for yourself!

Have you ever seen alien porn?

Um no what's that?

Just like a scene where an astronaut has sex with an alien

Um no

Like it's a dude dressed as an astronaut on some sound stage made to look like a spaceship and the alien is nothing more than a chick covered in green body paint with some prosthetic hands

Sounds like a kink

And then by the time they are done he has green paint all over his crotch and she has had all the paint rubbed off her pussy

Doesn't sound that appealing

It's not, just interesting what ppl like

That one falls under the category that ppl just like to see sex

In UFOlogy all of the abduction talk revolves around OB GYN exams by the aliens

Like in their flying saucers?

Yes, so a common thread, whether there is any truth to any of it or if it's some collective hype, is that the aliens like to perform aggressive gynecological exams on the females they abduct, this goes back to the 50s

Could it be certain women just looking for attention?

Maybe, or could it be that the aliens are most interested in human female reproductive systems, that life force that sustained earth for the last 200,000 years

Any reports of the aliens having sex with the women?

None of that, just being probed in big shiny exam rooms

Then what?

Then dropped back to wherever they were taken, in their bed or into their parked car

And with some lingering pain down there?

Yes, this is where skeptics jump in and say it's an imposed experience to replace actual sexual abuse perpetrated upon them

That's what I'm thinking too

I don't want to sound any crazier to you so I am going to say good night

Sleep well boo

You too

[Kawasaki Syndrome is an acute febrile illness of unknown cause that primarily affects children younger than 5 years of age. The disease was first described in Japan by Tomisaku Kawasaki in 1967, and the first cases outside of Japan were reported in Hawaii in 1976. Early stages include a rash and fever. Symptoms include high fever and peeling skin. In late stages, there may be inflammation of medium size blood vessels (vasculitis). It also affects lymph nodes, skin, and mucous membranes, such as inside the mouth. It's usually treatable with aspirin and intravenous immunoglobulin therapy given in a medical facility. Very rare]

["The Man" is a slang phrase that refers to the government or to some other authority in a position of power. In addition to this derogatory connotation, it may serve as a term of respect and praise]

[Club of Rome's professed mission is to "act as a global catalyst of change" by sponsoring studies and conferences and issuing reports and news releases that focus on long-term global problems and their interrelationships. The club is committed to an interdisciplinary perspective that highlights both the increasing interdependence of and problems among nation-states. From its first report titled The Limits to Growth, the Club of Rome has dedicated itself to identifying the most critical problems facing humanity; analyzing the interrelationships of these problems on the basis of an interdisciplinary, holistic, and global perspective; and positing future scenarios based on humanity's response to these problems. The club has identified a number of significant global issues, referred to as world problematique, facing humanity, including: depletion and pollution of the environment; demographic problems of both growth and aging; uneven development within and between nations; the decline of traditional values; dysfunctional governments; the quality and distribution of work; the sociocultural impact of new technologies; dysfunctional educational systems; the globalization of the economy; and international financial disorder]

[inoculation is the introduction of a pathogen or antigen into a living organism to stimulate the production of antibodies]

[Cosmic Pluralism is the belief that many worlds, planets, moons, and even the sun could contain life. It is a centuries-old philosophical belief that appeared heavily in Islam in the medieval era. Interpreting the texts of the major religions allows room for the expansion of the universe, the birth and death of stars, planetary formation, and evolution on Earth; it also makes room for life to exist on another planetary body. But the idea of intelligent life is the real challenge because humans are considered fallen human beings as (insert prophet) came to save the human beings not creatures on other planets]

[Space Force (USSF) is a military service that organizes, trains, and equips space forces in order to protect the USA and allied interests in space and to provide space capabilities to the joint forces. Other responsibilities include developing military space professionals, acquiring military space systems, maturing the military doctrine for space power, and organizing space forces]

[Goldilocks Planets are those planets which orbit in the habitable zone around a star, where temperatures like those on Earth occur, allowing for the possible existence of liquid water and of life]

[Star People refers to extraterrestrial life as a New Age belief that some individuals might have originated from another world or dimension]

[time space continuum is a mathematical model that joins space and time into a single idea called a continuum. This four-dimensional continuum is known as Minkowski space, and is used in cosmology to understand how the universe works on the biggest levels like galaxies, to the smaller levels like atoms]

[alien abduction probes are similar to human medical exams with minimal aesthetic sense. Alien medics attend to nude patients, the majority female, who are sedated by unknown forces and layed out in collapsed positions with their eyes rolled back and tongues out. Vital signs are constantly monitored, often out of a paranoia that the human may expire. Bedside manner has been described as brusque, clinical and task-oriented. Some abductees have reported that they did not mind the attention. Probing machines of varying shapes, sizes and design are inserted into the vaginal cavity, transmitting to handheld devices with medical information, most commonly fertility data]

DAY•FORTY ONE

Did you dream of me?

No, sorry

Any dreams?

No just thoughts

Like, of me?

No of the psychological torture we are all going through lmfao

It is getting exhausting

When you step back and look at it objectively it is one big exhausting cluster fuck

No wonder ppl want to stay isolated

There is that, but what gets me is the constant push and pull tugging on what to believe, and how to feel

I thought you were more cavalier than that

I am but I still have feelings

The ice queen is melting

It's more like all that gets revealed is put before you to try and process and that is what is tiring, crippling for some

Too much information all the time

Like I don't need to know my neighbor's politics on her social media, and somehow have that factor into my daily thoughts. Or some chick I went to high school with who now is a soccer mom and is a raging conspiracy theorist

I have a friend who I like immensely but he is so off with his politics now all I can think about is that he is nothing more than a stupid fuck lol

Sometimes the most simplified explanation is that they are just dumb, but then you think, am I the dumb one too?

It's like a form of impostor syndrome

Oh you remember that?

Yes but it's an offshoot of the dunning kruger effect, while you are willingly putting yourself into the mix

That is some serious meta awareness

And enlightenment

It is probably the most spiritually at ease that one can attain, simply knowing to be humble because your own scope is limited...and how much doesn't matter

That's why I could never be friends w ppl who would bloviate their opinions on any and all topics, with zero knowledge, just dropping misinformation

And now you see it online, you see it in the news, you see journalists doing it

We only suffer from it

When the news keeps being wrong do we at some point drown out the noise?

I'm getting there

And when the scientists with their projections are more off than a local weatherman do we stop following their predictions?

For many the answer is NO, more of a doubling down

It's cult thinking really

Doomsday mf'ers

There was a big doomsday cult out of Oakland who prophesied the complete end for the planet in 2011, their followers went all in during the lead up to that date. It seemed legit for many because it was explained this is when the Mayan calendar ended. What was required by the followers was a suspension in belief in order to go all in with the collective. Despite this 'church' leader, his name was Camping, having a history of incorrect predictions going back to the early 80s, he had predicted the end like a dozen times to no avail

Then what happened?

His followers sold all their stuff, ran up credit cards, bought from the church yard signs and t-shirts w their message, stood in front of stores, roamed subway stations telling ppl there was still time to be saved

And?

Then a week before 'The End" they sheltered in place, mostly in motels, and nothing happened

And their leader?

He explained it off as actually happening, that the believers were saved here on earth, and all others were now demonized

Wow

They stayed all in with him and his new message, then a year later, he was late 80s, he stroked out and died

And the followers?

They were buried in debt, and he became a prophet in death

Wtf, so twisted

This is kinda the mindset you need to know is out there when you see what is playing out around us

That's the struggle, trying to comprehend how we can all be so different, I get it, how we are raised is huge, and whatever else we are dealt

It's all part of the ingredients

And 'they' know it and that's how the marionette is played

They know our triggers

And what to dangle in front of us

Some of it is all the trauma survivors and their incapacity to process any emotional calculation without a full meltdown

It's funny sometimes I know exactly how someone is going to react to something, the predictability is hilarious

So it becomes all about emotionally charging people. And this virus or crisis is perfect for elevating the nerves then unleashing psychological warfare

That's what is exhausting

I'm exhausted talking about it

Me too

Time for wine?

Almost, just finished some yoga

Do tell

I did an extra 15 minutes and 3 new poses so my crotch got sweaty

You mean moist?

No, moist is very different than sweaty

Did you shower?

No I was thinking of staying like this all day

It's getting hot out there

Thank god for AC

Maybe this heat will kill the virus

Maybe, but if it does we won't know about it because we will only know what they want us to know

We sound like a couple of crusty old bitches bickering about society, get off my lawn mf'ers

At least we are keeping it real, would you like to be so woke that you seek out outrage in everything you see?

Um no, that's why I like you

Love you

Whoa 'love'?

Damn autocorrect

It's ok, you can say love

Well I guess at this point, what almost 2 months, it's not too soon

Love you

You too

• • •

Still in the yoga pants?

All day long and proud of it

No shame in your game

I like how they keep all the fat in its place

It can't be that bad

Honestly, it's not, but it's like wearing a push up bra for your legs and ass

Men need something like that, padded penis type thing

But that would be misleading, false advertising

Yes but in all likelihood it would just tease and nobody would actually find out

So like you walk around town, or sit in a park manspreading to show off a 70s rock god codpiece?

Kinda, to get the ppl worked up

Hot and bothered, then you ghost?

Pretty much, I mean c'mon, not gonna take some chick home then reveal the letdown

Letdown during lockdown

Exactly, if anyone is going to risk the virus there better be gold at the end of that rainbow

Maybe I could try it with my camel toe?

Um yes that would get quite the interest

Men are such horndogs I swear

Like I said days ago, WE ARE VISUAL

But do they realize that a camel toe kinda means a bigger pussy?

Do tell

Well the interior hole may be tight, but it means the girl either has a meaty majora because she is fat (it gets fat down there, just like boobs get bigger, when you are fat), or she just has a big one

Sounds appealing

But don't men just want it as small as possible, neat and proper?

Maybe but there is a fan club for everything

It's about personal taste I suppose, same w us, we don't necessarily want big dicks, in fact we are scared of them...give us something average and we are happy

That's not what we are led to believe

Stop watching so much porn, do you think they are going to put a small dick on the screen?

I guess not, you are watching exhibitionists who like to show off their exaggerated parts

Pretty much, while you take it all in amid isolation, hurried, horny, then the sudden let down

That feeling is often what keeps me from watching it, knowing it is a such a fleeting task that has guilt pang ramifications

It's only normal

I feel bad about the whole thing, like the actors especially

Wow that is deep

No seriously, I think they will look back and wonder what they were doing and regret it

But it's their choice sweety

I know but if there wasn't an audience there would be no demand and they wouldn't have to make it

That's really sweet but it's gonna exist with or without you

I just feel like I am part of the problem, in my own little way

So if I sent nudes would you feel better?

Say no more

Would you feel like you were exploiting me because you created the demand that wasn't there?

Um no, I'm sure there is demand outside of me

There, your logic is debunked

We could start off slow

Start what off?

The nudes, the rollout of nudes

Ok I was joking

It's ok, just start w something clothed then a small reveal

I was trying to make a point

Like a pic in a bra w you holding a newspaper from this week

Um why the paper?

To show me the nude is authentic

Honey if I send you something you better believe it's real

I just need verification

Like a hostage photo?

Yes, aren't we all hostages now?

What color bra?

You surprise me

No that wouldn't fly with your authentication, you tell me

Teal

Lmfao

Ok then a turquoise blue

Umkay, that's not a common color for bras

Okay white

I have a white sports bra, would you like that?

No, something lacey

Ok, plunging cleavage line or all-covering?

Purple with holes where the nipples go

Okay now it sounds like I am talking to a sex bot

That would just be like the most ideal scenario

How about red, with one strap down, like I am undressing for you?

Um how about no, you could just be describing some pic you got off the internet

Beggars can't be choosers

It's my fantasy now

Whoa, you ok?

Are we playing this out or not?

Not if you are going to be so aggressive

Sorry but the teasing is getting to me

Well I'm running out of wine so I don't know if I need to say goodnight so I can run to the market

Why, could we just resume after you get your booze

Cuz I'm not liking your tone tonight

I'm not liking your cocktease side

Cocktease? Oh, my bad

I think we should say goodbye

Bye boy

[cluster fuck: Military term for an operation in which multiple things have gone wrong. Related to SNAFU (Situation Normal, All Fucked Up) and FUBAR (Fucked Up Beyond All Repair). Its radio phonetic is Charlie Foxtrot]

[In the field of psychology, the Dunning-Kruger Effect is a cognitive bias in which people with low ability at a task overestimate their ability. It is related to the cognitive bias of illusory superiority and comes from the inability of people to recognize their own lack of ability]

[meta-awareness, or metacognition, is cognition about cognition, thinking about thinking, knowing about knowing, becoming aware of one's awareness and higher-order thinking skills. It can take many forms including knowledge about when and how to use particular strategies for learning or problem-solving]

[American Christian radio host Harold Camping stated that the Rapture and Judgment Day would take place on May 21, 2011, and that the end of the world would take place five months later on October 21, 2011. Camping presented several arguments labeled numerological, which he considered biblical proofs, in favor of the May 21 end time. A civil engineer by training, Camping stated he had attempted to work out mathematically-based prophecies in the Bible for decades, explaining, "I was an engineer, I was very interested in the numbers. I'd wonder, 'Why did God put this number in, or that number in?' It was not a question of unbelief, it was a question of, 'There must be a reason for it."]

[marionette: a puppet worked from above by strings attached to its limbs]

[woke: a political term of African-American origin referring to perceived awareness of issues concerning social justice and racial justice. It is derived from the African-American vernacular English expression "stay woke," whose grammatical aspect refers to a continuing awareness of these issues]

[manspreading is a term used by third-wave feminists to describe men who spread their legs (particularly on subway trains) to make room for their genitalia]

[cock tease: a girl who is flirtacious with almost any member of the opposite sex while pretending it is only innocent behavior, often with the primary intention of fishing for compliments]

DAY•FORTY TWO

So you're not going to say anything

Like what?

An apology or a semblance of one at least

For what?

Okay bye

Wait I'm sorry, did I do something?

It's not what you did, it was your tone last night, I don't like it

Too aggressive for you?

Yes and douchey, it didn't seem like you

I guess I was blinded by my horniess

Is that a thing now?

Yes it's always been a thing, horny rage

Is that so?

Yes so I am sorry for that, I wanted those nudes

That's gonna have to wait now, consider it a set back lol

Damn, sabotaging myself again

Besides, if you see something there will be less mystery

I think it's time

That's always what ppl think then it usually backfires

It won't for us

How do you know? How do I know you won't ghost me?

I would never ghost you, I need you more than you think

Ah that's sweet

If I didn't have you to talk to during lockdown I would go crazy

It is nice our little chat line isn't it?

Essential

DAY●FORTY THREE

The reason I won't send you nudes is the same reason I won't allow another woman into our bed

Um good morning, hi, it's me you're texting

I know

So not the wrong number?

Boo, what up with you? I know it's you, someone got your phone?

I'm just saying because you are talking about some other woman into our bed

Yes hypothetically I wouldn't allow it, not that it wouldn't be something hot, but it would be shattering to our core

Would you be jealous?

Yes and so would you

If you don't try it you can't knock it

Oh I have tried it and it always ends badly

Do tell

The jealousy becomes too much for everyone involved and relationships end over it

Like you wouldn't want to see some other girl pleasuring me?

No, and you wouldn't want to see me eating her pussy now would you?

I mean, it would be hot but no, hell no, not just jealousy but also some kind of inferiority complex would set in

Why?

Cuz we all know that women know how to eat pussy better than men

That's a myth, I mean there are some, but men can do it well too

It's hot but yeah I wouldn't want to jeopardize what we have

So for that same reason I don't send you nudes, I don't want to break what we have

A teaser can't hurt

But then where does the teaser lead?

Maybe to more pics

At some point it would need to end so why not just not start to begin with

This is what I mean by you being a royal tease

If that's what it takes

Takes what?

To keep you going

You don't need to tease me to keep me on here

Yes but I need to guide your attention

Like egg me along?

Yes that's how this works

This?

Erotic intrigue, the game, seduction, lasting friendship

Well I am willfully being played so there is that

• • •

Have you seen the talk of chip implants when all of this is over?

No, what?

Chip implants so the govt can monitor if you have a fever or if you have the virus or if you have come into contact w anyone who has it

No, that's not going to go over well

Well there is talk that it would be mandatory so going over well is not an option

People will revolt on that

You would hope, but if it's something mandatory in order to be out in public

That is sheeple thinking right there

What?

Not questioning how insane it is that the govt would implant you with a chip...this isn't some Tom Cruise sci-fi movie

I'm just sayin'

Saying what?

That if the govt wants it we will have to do it

That's not how it works

Look at the lockdown

People will be inconvenienced for a short while but I think that threshold is near, it's not going to last much longer with or without govt consent

I like that about you

What?

That determination, and spunk

Just telling you how it is boo

[talk of tracking chips to be implanted with a vaccine are mostly being debunked due to the technology not existing, at least what is known]

DAY•FORTY FOUR

I know we already talked about this void from all the celebrity and sports figure talk

No we haven't talked about that

Yes I swear we have

No must have been some other convo you are having

No, it was with you, anyway isn't it refreshing not having these assholes bloviating their virtue onto us

Who else are you chatting with?

Nobody really, just you, I mean some side chats with friends and co-workers

Okay just making sure you aren't getting me confused with someone else

Um I'm not going to get baited into one of your insecurity driven psycho dramas

I'm just saying if there are other 'friends' out there why don't you talk about them?

What and make you jealous?

No, just be real for a minute and tune me into what's going on in your life

What's going on in my life is that I am on lockdown and my main activity for the day is texting a complete stranger!!

Okay sorry I didn't mean to push it

What I was trying to say is that I do not miss-and this shows I never needed it-the guidance by celebrities in how I should live my life or think politically

It wouldn't matter either way if you didn't allow it to affect you regardless

Yeah I'm not led into thinking a certain way by them, but when it's everywhere in the ether at all times, with the same leaning and message, it tends to pull the masses into it

I have this new thing I'm doing

What's that?

If there is someone I do not like, like I cannot get with who they represent, when they then wax poetic and push their agenda, I play it that I would like to align with anything that is contrary to what they think

That's good

Ppl don't realize this because they tend to use big words, but actors are a dumb group, in fact, most never finished high school

Is that so?

Yes and same for athletes, even if they went to college they really didn't need to go to class, so it results with this fairly dumb and uneducated group who have a platform, able to voice opinions that do not matter, while being mostly out of touch from reality

Yeah fuck these assholes

LOL

I'm serious, who do they think they are?

They are smug and narcissistic so that results in them virtue signaling

I wonder how they are coping during lockdown knowing that nobody cares what they think

Yeah we got more important shit to worry about

So yeah we had a lighter version of this talk already, and I can see your growth

I will take that as a compliment

By all means

[58% of Hollywood actors do not have a high school diploma]

DAY●FORTY FIVE

What day are we now?

Wednesday, hump day

No, I mean what day of lockdown?

Like coming on 2 months

For real?

Yeah let's see, actually it's one and a half months

Did you pay all your bills?

Some

Which ones?

Cell phone lol

I paid my rent late just thinking maybe the landlord would offer me something

Just pay that shit and get on with it

He did come by last week, just after I paid it, and said he was up for trade of svcs, whatever that means

Are you fucking kidding me now?

No why?

Um that sounds illegal on many levels, you should turn him in

Wtf?

He comes over during a quarantine and tells you he is open to trade sex for rent, how is that not wrong?

He didnt say sex

He didn't have to

You think that's what he meant?

Yes, I know that's what he meant, it happens all the time

Wow

Yes, this is why landlords will often rent to hotter women with bad credit, they know they will fuck up again and the only thing that can save them is their pussy

Ewww

I wish guys had this problem

I'm sure there are some homo landlords

No I'm just saying, if there was a hot female landlord there would be dudes lined up to give some dick in lieu of rent

So I am paid up with money through the first, then I will reexamine the situation

Oh really

I mean I will see what's up with my work, maybe we will be off lockdown

I doubt it, but look that is just one more side effect of it all, sexual favors on creepers

Suicides, depression, alcohol abuse, anxiety, it's all there for the taking

Meanwhile we keep getting news that new parameters need to be met, that we are far from really flattening the curve

And that all the data to date has been wrong

There is that bullshit factor

I mean I guess nobody in this day and age can cop to being wrong

Oh never, it's this new thing called 'commitment signaling' - it's all about doubling down and going harder to signal to others, mostly within your tribe that you are devout with your convictions, even if you are wrong AF

Hilarious

What?

Wrong AF

Well that's what it is, and so many have been wrong on this whole pandemic, I don't think I have seen anything actually play out as predicted

But that's not what they want you to think nor acknowledge

First rule of being a virtue signaler, never admit you were wrong

You can justify anything by saying that's just 'how you feel'

Exactly, the last bastion FEELINGS

Like when you identify as something other than what you appear to be

Oh that's the 3rd rail of politics so we can't go there

It's a bubble they build then try and pull you into it, like a private safe space

The safe space is one big global clusterfuck at this point and they have pulled all of us into it

We need to unspin the web

There is lots to undo, it's like one step forward and then two back

I have faith there is some awakening on the horizon, something much bigger, that required a smaller event like this to trigger it

Smaller event like this??

It doesn't appear small now but looking back on it there is that possibility

A wrecked economy that may not recover will not look small

Do you realize that the last big pandemic was 1918 and then what happened 2 years later?

Idk what?

The beginnings of the roaring 20s - so let that sink in

Well we can't sustain ourselves on fiat money

I 'heard' we can as long as the economy bounces back and grows, it will swallow up that value added currency

Hot economics talk

Have you been drinking?

Maybe why?

Just trying to gauge if this conversation is headed somewhere else

Maybe why?

Off of virus talk

Maybe why?

Ok chat bot, text me later

●　●　●

If you die of the virus I will let your family know that your tombstone must read PLEASE SEND NUDES or your whole life was a lie

Lol

I mean think about it, isn't that your life's mission at this point?

I guess it's part of it but not everything

What do you think about when your libido wanes?

Like in my refractory period?

Your what period?

Like those moments right after you cum and you are overcome with that post coital bliss, the depleted energy

Yeah start there

It could be pangs of guilt if there was porn involved and what type of porn

I hope you're not talking animals or kids

Oh hell no, I'm talking like fat ppl or something like fisting

Ewww, I never understood that

Then that goes away and there are no thoughts of sex for a few hours

And then what do you think about?

Lately it's been how we are going to unwind from this

Then it's back to sex?

Kinda sorta

Like global conspiracy thinking then imagery flooding your mind of naked chicks

Perhaps it's like that - how about you?

I think about sex 24/7

Really, or is this just the wine talking?

It's always on my mind, like big dicks slapping my face, scruffy heads of men buried in my pussy, that sort of thing

Sounds like you don't have any time left to think about anything else

No just dicks in holes

[commitment signaling is a neologism for the conspicuous expression of commited values to a certain cause or set of morals. In evolutionary psychology and signaling theory, it is considered a natural behavior which may have either beneficial or detrimental effects at the collective level depending on various factors]

[The third rail of a nation's politics is a metaphor for any issue so controversial that it is "charged" and "untouchable" to the extent that any politician or public official who dares to broach the subject will invariably suffer politically]

[safe space: a place where individuals with cultural authoritarian and pro-censorship leanings go to in order to evade criticism while calling out whatever absurd ideas they may express, as well as ideas that are even slightly opposed to the safe space dweller's ideas, often with the intention to make the safe space occupant look like a victim]

[fiat money is currency established as money, often by government regulation, but that has no intrinsic value, as it does not have use value, but because the government maintains its value the parties engaging in exchange may agree on its valuation]

[refractory period refers to a period during the action potential, specifically the time during which another stimulus given to the neuron, regardless of how strong, will not lead to a second action potential]

DAY•FORTY SIX

What the fuck are we doing anyway?

Well good morning to you

Hi

Woke up on the wrong side again

Again?

I mean like first time

Ok snarky bitch

What we are doing is keeping each other uplifted during downtimes

But what if this is some manufactured bullshit meant to destroy us from within

That's deep...and a real possibility

It just seems like there is a underlying verve of near crisis tipping points

Like everybody is about to go off

Yes, not everyone but damn near

The sheeple are cool with it

Eventually they would go too, they might just be last

What is coming to light in the big reveal is the disparity and now even more than ever the truly lowest class

Like the homeless issue, I see them everywhere now

Include them into it, but I'm talking about minorities that have zero chance at opportunity, and the white trash

Real talk is that these ppl will never get jobs

Maybe they don't want them

Regardless they won't be getting them

White trash are funny in how they go full dunning kruger effect and fully embrace their identity, like they are the societal model of best life practices

Lmfao I always thought that too...I realized years ago they are happier than normies cuz they dont give a rat's ass

When the onion gets peeled like it is now, every day brings a new revelation, we glimpse into the collective soul and see it's bleak

For the working class too

Yeah but I think that ppl are content if they can make a good salary and consume

Just enough to get what you need, and then some, leaving everyone happy

Look at the big box retail, that whole caveman hunter-gatherer gene is fully on display, exercising that part of the reptilian brain

Then going into debt for it

Not everyone, sometimes it's all about spending exactly the amount you make

It's gross, just give me the basics and I am good

There is an opposing view to this in minimalism

So hot right now

Younger kids saw how debt wrecked their boomer parents, leaving behind mcmansions full of shit, and packed storage units

So much stuff that thrift stores are buried in it

And the irony is the hipsters are buying these clothes

Maybe costco is the manufactured opium of the people

Yes like a serotonin drip line of retail therapy

And those are the stores still opened during lockdown

Um, makes you wonder

While small retail is closed

Why would that be?

That's a good question nobody is asking

• • •

Is it happy hour yet?

It can be

I grant you full license to do your thang

Thang?

Thang y'all

Y'all?

Pardon my southern vernacular

Sounds like someone has already been drinking

Maybe

Ok BRB

• • •

It's not even like they are hiding it anymore

Hiding what?

The numbers

What numbers?

Of confirmed deaths

Are they secret now?

No they are not hiding that the numbers have been counted incorrectly

Do tell

Like if you have the virus and die of cancer it's counted as a virus death not a cancer death

Seems legit

Not really, that person would have died either way

Like they were on their deathbed?

Yes hospice, meaning they had stopped palliative care

Is it just a numbers grab?

Looks like it, either to bill more at the hospital, or for a political agenda by those counting the deaths

Why is it that we still believe what the govt tells us?

In Washington state it was revealed they counted the death of a guy who got gunned down in a robbery as a virus death

Did he have the virus?

Not clear, but he got shot in an armed robbery and they put him into the head count

If it's that bad then these numbers are way off

Yes it is that bad and the numbers are that off

Then this becomes a hoax?

If it's a manufactured hoax it is the biggest ever

If it's an accident?

Then it's a series of blunders so epic that it exposes how weak the system really is

Maybe it's more nefarious than that

Let me get my tinfoil hat

Like it's a test run, or it's to try out how much the public is willing to take

Or it takes our eyes off of something else

Away from the prize

But that's just the hamster wheel

Right, as we drone on with our lives chasing butterflies and unicorns

What about porn?

And that

Feeding the beast, chasing the dragon, getting off by signaling into the echo chamber of your own narcissistic palace of complacency

Wow

It's kinda how we structure the world around us and create the devices to fill the needs

Like a cockpit with certain controls

A custom crafted nest

Like how cities are the most advanced nest known to mankind and society

I guess

No, what I mean is that an elaborate big city is the physical manifestation of all the best of society fully built out, played out, tested and true...the infrastructure, the traffic patterns, the entertainment, the leisure and the commerce

Like that, but now crafted within your mind. This becomes how you see the world. What they call rosy glasses. It becomes your narrow vision, then this gets applied to the larger world, if you so choose to

We are seeing more of it now

Like masks and the controversy associated with wearing one or not

That just seems to be a gullibility test

Maybe, but it now is a physical manifestation of someone's thinking that you would have never known

They are giving themselves away

You can see it like that, but for them they are broadcasting that they care or some shit

The new mask truth is that they don't help at all

Lmfao tell that to the mask nazis

Well think about it, if this virus is so lethal and aggressive it's gonna penetrate the mask, especially if you are wearing it under your nose, or if it's some bandana

But doesnt it look cool LOL

Not really, and that's one more reason that I am going out less, I just don't like to see it

It's all about the virtue, and then the alignment politically falls into place

I'm over it

It may not be going anywhere

You see, it's a visual reminder that the virus is still here and a threat

Without the masks that fear subsides

[snarky: crotchety, snappish, sarcastic, impertinent, or irreverent in tone or manner]

[hunter-gatherer, also called forager, any person who depends primarily on wild foods for subsistence. Until about 12,000 years ago, when agriculture and animal domestication emerged in southwest Asia and in Mesoamerica, all peoples were hunter-gatherers]

[thang: nonstandard spelling of thing representing southern US pronunciation, and typically used to denote a feeling or tendency]

[BRB, be right back, used when talking to someone you care about and don't want them to go away, while you have something urgent that needs immediate attention, say 'brb', but make sure you don't make them wait too long]

[tinfoil hat theory: tin foil hats are made from one or more sheets of aluminium foil, or a piece of conventional headgear lined with foil, often worn in the belief or hope that it shields the brain from threats such as electromagnetic fields, mind control, and mind reading]

[rosy glasses refers to optimism and the tendency to see things in a positive light, while rosy retrospection is the tendency to view past events in a positive, yet often unrealistic light]

DAY•FORTY SEVEN

When I walk out into the glaring sunlight and out of the cool AC I feel that I need that heat and sun and that it's not the most ideal conditions for a virus

But haters will say the virus likes the heat

But realists will say virus season is in the cold of winter, so what is it?

It can be both they would say, depending on the virus, and this one in particular likes heat

So how is it doing in the Sahara desert?

Let me check...and it's not there

And when I stretch and move and flex in the sun and feel the sweat forming on the low of my back this feels right

And your sweaty cameltoe?

That feels right too

If you look up vitamin D, which only comes from sunlight, studies have shown it kills this virus

How do we know who to believe?

I would go with whoever has been wrong the least amount of time

LOL then factor some other calculation into that and you might be near the truth

Didn't you know, this is a post-truth world?

Well it's Saturday and nice out so lemme text you later

● ● ●

I started keeping one of those prison style calendars, marking off the number of days

I'm glad you're back

So without a date for the end, I just count up

No release date from the prison sentence

I'm up to 47 days and I don't know if that's right, it seems longer

Sounds right

But that's not even 2 months, this shit seems like a year

It'd be nice if we could count down to something

Knowing a return to normal life date would be helpful

But then the excitement would be gone

You mean the mystery in not knowing

Yes, it would take away from all the questions, and the power of the politicians

Don't get me started

It really is about the politicians at this point

Yes, not so much the virus

They are the ones deciding how we react

And we could take another approach, like in the past, where you let the virus play out on its own within the playbook of nature

Like get to herd immunity?

Yes if that's what it takes, or let it weaken or even flame up then flame out

Flame out lol I think of some virus acting all gay

Heyyyyy

[post-truth world is a culture in which debate is framed largely by appeals to emotion disconnected from the details of policy, and by the repeated assertion of talking points to which factual rebuttals are ignored]

[As viruses do not like sunlight, high temperatures and humidity, this virus will likely flame or burn out this summer. Sunlight cuts the virus' ability to grow in half so the half-life will be 2.5 minutes and in the dark it's about 13 to 20. The virus can remain intact at 4 degrees celsius (39 degrees Fahrenheit) or 10 degrees (50 F) for a longer period of time. At 30 degrees (86 degrees F) you then get inactivation. And high humidity is an unsustainable environment for any type of virus]

DAY•FORTY EIGHT

My eyes are beginning to look like dark sinkholes

It can't be that bad

Dehydration and lack of sun have wreaked havoc on my skin

Pics or it didnt happen

Like a leathery look, almost as if something is happening internally

I hope you are okay, take care of yourself

Perhaps it's organ malfunction, maybe my thyroid, or diet

If you know you are not right then you are not

Something is up and it's not just a girl thing

I'm not an OBGYN but I could take a look

Lmfao disgusting

Do you have insurance? Can you go to an urgent care?

I'm not walking into a hot zone

And expose yourself to the virus?

Yes I can't put my immune system through that

Do you have any of these infamous 'co-morbidities'?

Not really, like obesity or diabetes?

Yeah or high blood pressure

Negative, you know me, I live a healthy lifestyle except my wine

Can you type your symptoms into a medical site and see what comes up?

Too scared, ok boo it was nice talking to you but I gotta run some errands

Okay don't ghost me

Never

DAY•FORTY NINE

Good morning

DAY•FIFTY

Hi

DAY•FIFTY ONE

Just reply back that you are okay, that's all I ask

DAY•FIFTY TWO

Hey, boo here, not wanting to sound clingy or anything but hit me back

DAY•FIFTY THREE

I miss you, but honestly I'm really worried now

DAY•FIFTY FOUR

If I could have any dream it would be to text with you again

DAY•FIFTY FIVE

If you are ghosting me then this has all been a cruel hoax

DAY•FIFTY SIX

I don't want to come off as insecure cuz I know that is a huge turn off

DAY•FIFTY SEVEN

Okay it seems like you need space, whatever you need

DAY•FIFTY EIGHT

Just hit reply w a smiley face or some corny shit

DAY•FIFTY NINE

What day are we on, can you tell me from your prison calendar?

DAY•SIXTY

Did you see the news about the modified restrictions? Yay, this is good news

DAY•SIXTY ONE

And if you missed that, the news about the virus being less dangerous than the flu, now it's confirmed

DAY•SIXTY TWO

Everything you had predicted has played out, you are wise beyond your years

Umkay, hi

Whoa you are there?

Yes, just getting back to you real quick

What's been going on?

Quite a bit actually

So you weren't...um...ghosting me?

No, but my focus needs to be redirected for now

Sad face

It's not about you, it's about me

That's what they always say

Well that's because it's true

Do we still have a chance?

Chance?

You know, to keep talking, maybe meet up

I don't know if there is time unfortunately

I don't mean today, I'm saying when all of this is over

Again, what part of time do you not understand?

Time, a measurement of progress along some linear line

Ok wise guy

Are you making big plans for after the lockdown?

Making plans but if you call survival big then yes

We will all survive this

I have cancer

Whoa what?

Ok I am not going to keep retyping what I just wrote because you are not following along

Sorry

So like I was saying I have cancer. It's news to me. It's rare and aggressive

I'm speechless now

Me too

And I'm crying, just want you to know that

Thank you but more sad sympathy isn't what I need

You will fight this and win

Or that bloviating nonsense too

Sorry, it's just that now I'm a wreck and I don't know what to say

Your silence is appreciated

DAY●SIXTY THREE

Good morning

DAY•SIXTY FOUR

I hope you are feeling okay today

DAY•SIXTY FIVE

If you can, let me know your battle plan

DAY•SIXTY SIX

I will leave you alone for now, hit me up whenever you feel like talking

DAY•SEVENTY FIVE

You know what really pisses me off?

Hey, what's that?

All the scare tactics they deployed on us, all that wasted fear that was exhausting and based on lies

Pretty much

And now when I face a true horror, the challenge of my life, the fear of immortality I would like that energy back, it's almost like now I have no real fear left, only a cloud of exhaustion

It's bullshit

The abject certitude needed to survive a very real illness, something that isn't being blown up in the media or weaponized by politicians

They are all motherfuckers

I want that energy back, I want that time back, I want to go back where I would have seen a doctor earlier

Now we just need you to focus on the future

There isn't much of one for me

Is there anything you are not telling me?

Yes lots but I don't want to scare you

Please we have come this far I have some right to know

It's not something I can survive

Sure you can

No listen to me, I cannot

You aren't even going to try

Bye

DAY●SEVENTY SIX

Sorry about being so pushy last night hope you're feeling better today

DAY•SEVENTY SEVEN

Hi just a quick note to say I am thinking about you

DAY•SEVENTY EIGHT

I believe you, I want you to be okay, please send me a signal

DAY•SEVENTY NINE

What I was trying to tell you is that I'm not gonna make it. And that I'm okay with that. It took some processing but I think it's time

Whoa, please don't talk like that

Don't tell me how to talk

Sorry

Experts have deemed it, me, as a lost cause

What are we talking about?

Days

Um, WITAF?

Yes days

Are you in a hospital?

Fuck no, my system is too weak for that, they even advised I return home

Cuz of the virus?

Yes they said if I got it in the hospital, or from a nurse, or another patient, I will be dead in 48 hours

That is some high drama shit

Yes it is, that's why I'm home now

I want to bring you the best care package in the history of care packages

That's nice but I can't have visitors

Rules are made to be broken

Not this time

I could just drop it off

Are you trying to kill me?

No why?

The contamination

[WITAF: what in the actual fuck]

DAY•EIGHTY

That internal desire to eat a bat

Good morning, where is this going?

To then search it out in a wet market

If that's what really happened

Let's just say it is official

Ok I will suspend judgment

Then that walk to the market, and the day before that, when the exotic animal hunter killed the bat in the jungle

I guess there are those dudes

Who brings it back and presents the bat for purchase

Are you okay?

The sick fuck who takes it home and cooks it

Yeah gross AF

Then the virus inside the bat penetrating dinner boy's system, mainlining his bloodstream, infecting him with some new animal to human transmission

Pretty much

Then he wakes up the next day to a bad flu, coughing with respiratory issues but blames it on his heavy cigarette diet

Everyone smokes in China

He meets up with friends in the city center and coughs up a storm, he infects a dozen people

Where are you going with this?

They all go home and infect everyone in their govt housing

This could be very much how it initially played out

What's the alternative?

Manufactured by the Communist Party, weaponized

It spreads to several hundred people then thousands within days, some begin flying internationally

It took weeks before travel was shut down

The strain was then splattered across the globe, scientists got involved, models were projected, and lockdowns were ordered

And here we are?

The disruption to the system, the sheltering to avoid a spread, the avoidance of hospitals and timely diagnosis

All the deaths of elderlies

All that went unnoticed by the distraction

You are in that boat

While a virus of its own spread in my body

A small local act, something not uncommon, spread a global displacement within weeks

Like how a butterfly's flapping wing can trigger a hurricane on the other side of the world

Now we are all linked, whether we like it or not, by a chain of events

And anyone who wants to can rattle the chain

Or cut off a link

DAY●EIGHTY ONE

Like how the cancer inside me broke off the tumor then was carried through my lymph system

The metastasis?

Yes thank you. Into my bones, into my liver, into my lungs

I am so sorry

It's this rippling effect, like a wildfire

You will be okay

DAY●EIGHTY TWO

Everything has an end

Without an end there can be no beginning

And without shadows there is no light

This will end too, the lockdowns

I would like that more than anything

Tastes of freedom, and a small semblance of a life before all of this

You will see it

I can't see how we unwind from this, how it's become so political

The business shutdowns, it's not so easy to flip the switch back on

Church closures, shutting down beaches

The fallout when this is wrapped up

I don't see how it will be put back into the bottle

We know the emperor has no clothes

And the genie is out of the bottle

Like trying to squeeze a shit back into your ass

Ewww

I can't imagine how this is undone

Like the spread of my cancer

DAY•EIGHTY THREE

Check the news

What's up now?

I think we have the bow tie to wrap this all up

The butterfly wings fluttering?

Yes

Do tell

Video of a white cop killing a black man

Another shooting?

No, he has his knee on the guy's neck

DAY•EIGHTY FOUR

Overnight riots, they burned down a police precinct

The virus wasn't enough

Looks like it

It wasn't punching its weight in the Grim Reaper department

It's like the virus had been infected with its own more dangerous virus, and that virus took over

The loneliness affects us in different ways

New lines have been drawn, invisible ones

Those we dare not cross

Mental borders

Emotional barricades

New channels for getting off

No longer the conventional means of a pre-virus existence

That world is gone

The FOMO is strong for these rioters

For some it's a block party

Or a free for all black friday

Who can blame them really?

It's like the govt kept us on the edge for months now it's time to jump

When I think I have gone mad I find comfort in knowing I have you

Same for me boo

I'm always here for you

When I was a child they told me it was okay I talked to my stuffed animals, to give them names and make conversation

It's good for the imagination they said

It's like taking on the role of the parent-like relation

Real life friends don't always cooperate

They may not share, or they could talk too loud

Or not go home when asked

Having an imaginary friend doesn't necessarily mean you are troubled

Quite the contrary

They are the best source of comfort during difficult times

And helpful in coping with trauma

Don't forget, you can blame them for misbehavior

Why hold down such a magical expression

It's the theory of mind at play

And that is proof alone of your own social intelligence

That you can understand someone other than yourself may want something different

Even for things you didn't know about

Self-determination theory

Relatedness, competence, autonomy

These stories may be made up to not intrude upon others

Or a way to take some control back

What the professionals call private talk

Self-talk to calm ourselves down

For now we have each other

To keep us sane and intact

And to learn from each other

When we don't need each other we will know, right?

When that time comes it will be goodbye

For now it's totally okay, right?

We are okay...

Acknowledgements:

For her enormous heart and compassion, my wife. She provides for a wonderful life that affords me a great gift, that of time to write.

About the Author:

American writer Tennison Long is the author of Glorious Verve, When We Ran The Master Plan, Of Tribe & Empire, On Becoming Yesterday's Actors, tex•tu•al, How to Fake Your Death (& Other Illusions of Exile), and The Devolution. He likes to take his readers on a psychological thrill ride, blending the macabre with the sublime while sewing seams of mental confusion with emotional clarity. He offers a uniquely imagined prose that sustains moments of sputtering haunted brilliance. He lives in Northern California and would love to hear from you.

Visit his website at www.tennisonlong.com